THE VELVET GLOVE

Set in the earliest years of the twentieth century, this is the story of two marriages evolving from different social backgrounds. Central to the theme of love and tragedy are Rick Ferris, a business tycoon, and the passionate, rebellious Kate Barrington whom he marries, whilst there is also the inevitable sadness of the union of the elusive waif-like Cassandra and Jon, heir to an aristocratic family.

THE VELVET GLOVE

THE VELVET GLOVE

by

Mary Williams

Magna Large Print Books
Long Preston, North Yorkshire,
BD23 4ND, England.

British Library Cataloguing in Publication Data.

Williams, Mary
　　The velvet glove.

　　　A catalogue record of this book is
　　　available from the British Library

　　　ISBN　　0-7505-1484-1

First published in Great Britain by Robert Hale Ltd., 1994

Published in Large Print 2000 by arrangement with Mary Lewis

Magna Large Print is an imprint of Library Magna Books Ltd.

Printed and bound in Great Britain by
T.J. (International) Ltd., Cornwall, PL28 8RW

Author's Note

The characters and events portrayed in *The Velvet Glove* are fictitious except for a single reference to Lady Jane Grey, the 'nine days' queen. However, the area depicted as 'Burnwood Forest' is meant to capture the atmosphere of Charnwood Forest, which is to be found in the very centre of England. I have used local landmarks, hamlets, and adjoining towns under different names for the sake of the story-line. Anyone knowing the district will no doubt find many recognizable, despite certain juggling with geography. Beacon Hill exists, and Bradgate.

Should any reader be tempted to explore the secret valleys, woodlands, and narrow lanes winding beneath rocky tumps of hills, I hope something of the magic I always found there is sensed and reborn.

Times change.

I hear new roads have been built in the vicinity and buildings have sprung up eroding several former beauty spots, but much of the Forest – call it 'Burnwood' or the real Charnwood – still exists and is protected by law for the benefit of wild life, and human beings who still in this industrial age cherish Nature's gifts – almost mystical – that are our heritage.

Mary Williams (Lewis) 1994

Prologue

The moment she entered the Tree Studio it seemed to Kate that Cassandra's personality emanated and gathered force as a single personality.

Gentle elegance blended subtly – almost slyly – with the haphazard untidiness of a shawl lying crumpled over the narrow divan in one corner, a pair of sandals on the floor, books in a disordered pile on the wicker table and a blue cape hanging on a peg. Paints and an unfinished watercolour sketch of a tree with imaginary faces half-suggested through the branches had been pushed on a low shelf against the wall. Make-up had rolled from a half-open handbag, including a lipstick now lying on the colourful Oriental rug. There was an expensive-looking hanging mirror facing the open door that, in the changing late afternoon, gave a strange impression of reflected movement emphasized by the shapes of trees swaying fitfully through the glass. The air was heady, soft and sultry, holding the scent of wood, and damp leaves blending nostalgically with something else – a lingering faint perfume – Cassandra's.

And as she stood motionless staring through the quivering pattern of light and shade, Kate started remembering.

In a kaleidoscope of events the past swam through her mind. She shivered, and was unaware of the crackling of a man's feet on the twigs and encrusted earth behind her, until his voice suddenly penetrated her senses.

She turned and saw Rick's face – lean, dark-eyed staring down on her.

'I thought I might find you here,' he said. 'But there's no point in brooding. The past's over. Done with.'

'Such a waste.'

'Nothing's a waste,' he told her, with a touch of grimness. 'I guess we've learned a few things, you and I.'

'We oughtn't have had to.'

'Come along. We're going home. You've a

family. Remember?'

Of course she remembered. She remembered everything the good and the bad, the happy and the sad – all the intricate events leading to this moment when Cassie, for a few brief seconds, seemed to be very near. As they walked back to the carriage waiting down the lane, her thoughts automatically switched back to the point long ago when she'd first got involved with Rick Ferris in 1905.

It was the occasion of the dance at Charnbrook Hall where she'd worn the crimson dress for the first time.

Yes, that exotic attire had started it all and settled the courses of four lives – hers and Rick's, Cassandra's and Jon's. And it had been at *her* will. She alone had been responsible.

Or had she?

1

Walter Barrington and his wife Emily were gratified when their only child, a daughter, Kate, was invited to the birthday dance of a school friend, Isabella Wentworth. It proved that the considerable expense of her education at the most select boarding-school in the country had been worth while.

The Wentworths after all were of that elite breed, the English aristocracy; the son of the house, the Honourable Jonathan, would become, on the death of his bachelor uncle, Lord Wynterley. In the meantime, any connection of the Barringtons with Isabella's family was a step towards bridging the polite but mostly impregnable class-barrier existing in those early years of the century between Trade and the Gentry.

Walter did not consider himself a snob, nor even a 'climber'. He was stolid middle class, and proud of it, having inherited a

13

considerable fortune from his father, in the stocking trade, furthered by his own needle-sharp mind for finance and an enviable capacity for cunning investments and understanding of stocks and shares.

It was natural, therefore, that he should wish the very best for his only child.

His estate and country mansion were situated seven miles from the industrial city of Lynchester on the outskirts of the Burnwood Forest, with only six miles dividing the house and lands from those of the Wentworths which stretched towards Larchborough on the opposite side of the picturesque woodland area.

So, should any romantic friendship arise between Isabella's brother and Kate, social contact would be easily accessible.

Walter had a shrewd idea that Kate's interest was wandering in the right direction. The two young people had already met at charity functions organized by Lynchester's Lady Mayoress, and since that first occasion he'd noticed a tell-tale gleam in his daughter's lovely eyes whenever the Wentworth name was mentioned.

Although she'd professed indifference at any teasing quip concerning the Hon. Jon, Walter knew he'd hit the mark. Kate was proud. But if she fancied the young lord-to-be, he'd do his damnedest to see she got what she wanted. He had the cash, and the Wentworths, from all accounts, were in need of it. Blue blood didn't pay taxes and bills, which was where he could be of assistance.

Kate was a good-looking girl, and a character, full of bounce and the joy of life; in her parents' eyes a credit to the name of Barrington, capable of bringing new vitality to any fading top-notch family she married into.

A spot of fresh healthy blood was necessary from time to time for the continuance of good stock in any noble tree, Walter told himself, and the Wentworths were no exception. It was just a matter of encouraging every chance there was of seeing they realized it.

No open bribery of course; his own integrity and pride in his daughter wouldn't resort to that. But there were ways – there

15

were ways. A lessening of financial strain for the future could be a heartwarming and helpful stepping-stone in establishing friendly relationships – even if they were needed, which shouldn't be necessary where a lovely girl like Kate was concerned.

Emily, who well knew the trend of her husband's thoughts, was more cautious.

'Don't try and force things, Walter,' she said. 'Kate will know her own mind when the right time comes along. She's got a brain and heart of her own.'

Actually Kate already knew.

She wanted Jon.

On their first brief meeting at the civic garden party she had sensed a quick rapport between them with a leap of excitement that on her part was rather more. Jon had such charm, he was so handsome: tall, with that certain fair-haired, blue-eyed air of gallantry and dedicated attention that imbued her fleetingly with a sensation of romance.

It was true they had found very little to say to each other, but time and opportunity had been so limited. He'd been in great demand.

Naturally.

But his expression had been full of admiration and, before being dragged away by some pushy society female, he'd said, smiling, 'It's been ripping meeting you, Miss Barrington, Izzy must bring you to Charnbrook one day. I'll look forward to that.'

She'd been aware of his glance travelling under lowered lids over the gauzy frill of tulle at her neck to her tiny waist and voluminous drapes below. The shade was of soft blue. Not her shade really, with her rich colouring – cream, glowing skin, full red lips and dark amber-gold eyes shining brilliantly under her flowered but tasteful hat; it had been her mother's choice. She felt a swift flush stain her cheeks, and pushed a rebellious strand of copper-bright hair from a cheek.

'Thank you,' she'd said, adding with a quick flurry of words, 'yes, I'd like to – very much.'

'See you remember.'

He'd moved away with one arm dragged by the odious blonde.

Had he really meant it? she'd wondered

afterwards, or was it mostly politeness on his part?

If she'd known Isabella better she'd have pumped her and found out, but the two girls had only really become friendly during a brief period at finishing-school. Anyway, the ice was broken now. Somehow, Kate decided, she'd find or make an excuse for renewing the contact.

As things turned out the necessity hadn't arisen.

The dance had solved matters, and this time she'd chosen her own gown. She was old enough, good heavens. Eighteen. Nearly nineteen. Mama would have to listen.

Mama had been forced to.

Hence the crimson dress.

It was of seductive shimmering satin, temptingly *décolleté* on the shoulders above the tightly fitting bodice. Slightly below the waist folds were drawn to the back then left to flow freely in a billowing circle to the points of silver slippers. Staring at her image through the long cheval mirror in her bedroom Kate felt a leap of excitement. She looked not only beautiful, but more mature suddenly, with an exotic quality that would surely titillate Jon Wentworth's senses. In a wave of self-revelation she recognized she had never in her life wanted anything or anyone so much. Would he respond? Oh, he must, he must, she thought, humming a bar or two of the 'Blue Danube' softly under her breath. Her body swayed rhythmically from side to side, both hands lifting the full skirt slightly above her ankles. Her head was tilted upwards on her slender neck, flower-like, with her massed hair rich and glowing in the transient light from the window.

A creak of the door startled her. She turned, as Emily entered the room.

'Is this a rehearsal?' she queried in faintly acid tones. She loved Kate and was proud of her. But there had been moments recently when she'd considered her daughter was becoming too conscious of her own charm and good looks.

'Yes,' Kate answered shortly. 'It's only a week to the dance now, and I wanted to be sure everything was all right.'

'Didn't we arrange for the neckline to be slightly raised at the last fitting? Mrs Adams quite agreed with me it would be better, if you remember.'

'But she's a bit of a fuss-pot, Mama. And *you're* a bit old-fashioned, you know. In society these days colour and style are important. So I called on her the other day when I was in Lynchester and told her to leave it as it was.'

'You did that? Without telling me?'

Kate sighed. 'Mama! I'm eighteen years old. Not a schoolgirl any more. The Wentworths will expect any friend of Isabella's to be up-to-date. So please – *please* don't criticize. It's a *lovely* dress, and I'll love wearing it. Now do smile. Say you like it. Honestly! – I do know what's fashionable and what's not. You can't say it doesn't suit me. Or shall we ask Papa's opinion?'

'You look smart, I suppose,' Emily agreed grudgingly, knowing that as Walter would undoubtedly side with his daughter, any more protests would be useless. 'But I'd have preferred something more modest myself. Still, it's your dance – your friend's I should say. I only hope you're right about the Wentworths' taste, and that they won't think you look the slightest bit – cheap.'

Kate laughed; a merry sound.

'Dear Mama. You are funny. Cheap? When I'm going to wear your diamond pendant? You did *promise*. Remember?'

Shaking her head, Emily threw up her hands. 'You're impossible, Kate.'

'But you *do remember?*'

'Of course. I said you could borrow it, and I keep my word. But I think you should give a thought to Cassie. All your finery's going to put her in the shade more than ever. I shall have to look through my jewel case and find something special for her. In my opinion it's a pity Isabella included her in the invitation. She'll probably feel quite out of things.'

Kate thought so too.

Just at that point the presence of Cassandra Blacksley at Beechlands looked something of a hindrance and a boring obligation to shoulder. She was the adopted daughter of a cousin of Walter's, the widow of a minister living in Yorkshire. The child had been taken in by the couple when she was six years old, but two years later Wilf

Blacksley had died leaving his wife and the little girl very little to live on. Walter had done his best from time to time to be of financial help; but his relative, possessing more than a fair share of the Barrington stubborn pride, had been fiercely independent and started a small dressmaking business in Bradford, which she ran with sufficient efficiency to support the two of them. One suggestion of Walter's she agreed to was that Cassandra, a rather frail girl, should spend six weeks of every summer at Beechlands to gain benefit from the country air and change of scene. When they were young children, before Kate went away to school, the two had been companionable. Kate had quite enjoyed playing the role of youthful fairy-godmother to poor Cassie who had to live in such bleak circumstances. But in their late teens the difference of backgrounds and interests had widened. Cassandra had seemed to withdraw more into herself and become even less colourful in looks and character. She was a slight pale girl with little to say for herself, and seldom laughed or saw a joke. What good points she had physically faded and went unnoticed in Kate's exuberant company; her large black-lashed luminous grey eyes failed to register. Her abundance of fine straight hair worn severely in a knot at the back of her small head appeared merely nondescript mouse, although in sunlight it could brighten transiently to tawny gold. Kate considered her plain; but her features were small and finely chiselled; there was an elusive quality about her generally ignored – too secretive for most people to bother about or even be aware of.

Her true background was not referred to by the Barringtons; it was doubtful even that Walter's cousin knew her exact heredity. She had been adopted from an orphanage when the minister and his wife learned they could never have children of their own. Through the years her identity had been completely accepted as Cassandra Black-sley. Cassandra, because she had been so labelled at the institution where she'd lived since babyhood. None of the family delved any more into those far past years. Even Kate never wondered about her beginnings.

She was just her rather remote and unfortunate second cousin whose company had to be endured at intervals during the summer months. With her natural warm-heartedness Kate had tried intermittently to make Cassie's visits enjoyable. But the effort had become increasingly boring. Whereas Kate enjoyed socializing, using the carriage or new motorcar to be driven into Lyn-chester for a shopping spree, and physical exercise like walking the dog or riding her mare, Beth, over the countryside bordering the Forest, Cassandra preferred 'mooning about' – Kate's expression – with a drawing pad and box of water colours to make sketches of trees and wild flowers. Kate thought the results rather colourless, like Cassie herself, although Emily said the paintings showed talent for detail, and had imagination.

'If she'd had training and gone to art school,' she said to Walter one day, 'she might have turned out to be a really good artist.'

'Well, my dear, I did offer to foot the bill,' Walter pointed out, 'but you know how pigheaded that cousin of mine is. And the girl will be a good help in that little business of hers. It's not for us to interfere.'

'No, I suppose not.'

So matters were left as they were, and no one had grudged Cassandra's summer months at Beechlands until the year of Isabella's dance, when Kate was to wear the red dress.

Everything could have been so wonderful, she thought, if she hadn't to be burdened with Cass. But in a careless moment she'd mentioned her presence to Isabella, and Isabella had insisted she'd bring her along with her.

'But you *must*,' she'd said. 'Your cousin? Of course she must come. It will be my last chance of meeting her probably. I'm going to India next month to be married. It would be frightfully hurtful to leave her out. Yes. It's *my* dance. And I'm *asking* her, here and now, unless you want me to write. Do you?'

'No. Of course not,' Kate had agreed reluctantly. 'Although I don't know what she'll wear. She hasn't brought a wardrobe of dresses with her.'

'There are shops in Lynchester. Or had you forgotten?'

'No, all right. As you say. We'll fix something up.'

The 'fixing up' had been comparatively easy.

It had been decided that Kate's blue chiffon with a few small alterations and tucks and stitches would suit Cassandra very well. The idea had been Kate's.

'I've only worn it that once at the garden party,' she'd pointed out to Emily. 'It isn't really *my* style, and you know how funny Aunt Blacksley is about spending money on anything for Cass. And anyway it would be a shame to waste it – it's a pretty dress, just right for someone small and fair like her.'

There was nothing intentionally patronizing in Kate's remark. It was merely that the thought of a whole afternoon having to be spent in the town choosing something for Cassandra bored her.

So matters were arranged. Cassandra had accepted the invitation although Kate had hoped she wouldn't, and on that special evening as the girls dressed for the event, the only real cloud on Kate's horizon was the looming picture of having to usher her dull cousin around, help find her partners, which would inevitably interfere with any chances she had of concentrating her complete attention in gaining the notice and admiration of the Hon. Jon.

However, when the time came and the two girls walked down the terrace steps to the great Daimler motorcar waiting to take them to Charnbrook, excitement momentarily drove any niggling thought of Cassandra from Kate's mind. The vehicle had been recently purchased by Walter, although the family carriage was still retained and the two greys kept in the stables.

Emily, who still mildly distrusted motors, had exclaimed, 'I don't really like the idea; think of the way your friend's son, Archie Plummer, poor boy, landed in a ditch the other day. Fancy! – having to *crawl* out! It would be dreadful if anything like that happened to the girls!'

'Couldn't!' Walter had stated firmly. 'That was a two-seater! A *Ford*. This is the best –

large and firm. Good engine and gears. Real works. Fit for a king. They'll be all right. Adam knows his job.'

Adam was the man, once a mechanic in Barrington's employ, who'd specially trained to be chauffeur. He was middle-aged, sturdy, and competent to crank the engine and change a wheel in case of a mishap.

Kate didn't care what transport was used. All that concerned her was to look her best when she arrived at the Wentworths. Of course, the motor would probably be quicker, provided it didn't have a puncture or breakdown of any kind *en route*, and that was hardly likely; Adam had spent the whole afternoon seeing everything was in order, and they'd take the Larchborough main road for a good deal of the way instead of the quiet maze of cross-country lanes, usually used by the carriage. The Daimler would certainly give a stylish touch to their arrival.

Everything was going to be wonderfully exciting. Nothing was to mar the evening ahead. Except perhaps – Cassie.

As the large car purred – or perhaps grunted was a better word – along the newly macadamised road surface – Kate took a doubtful glance at her cousin. She was wearing a borrowed blue velvet cape to match the dress, and was sitting quietly with her pale face sunk into the fur-lined collar. Rather nondescript as usual, Kate thought, although her hair looked quite pretty – pale and goldish, arranged on top. Kate, who was wearing sumptuous black in dramatic contrast to the striking red, wanted to give her a dig, but merely said, with just a hint of irritation in her voice, 'Buck up, Cass. We're going to *enjoy* ourselves tonight. There's nothing to gloom about. You look quite nice, you know. Blue suits you.'

'Does it?'

'Well – don't you think so?'

'Oh, well, in a way, perhaps. Only it's *your* dress; it makes a difference.'

'It isn't mine any more. It's yours.'

'Yes, I know. You're very kind, Kate. Don't worry; I'll try not to embarrass you.'

'What do you mean?'

'Don't think of me as a responsibility. Of

having to find me partners, I mean.'

Kate flushed, lifted her chin stubbornly and stared through the car window at the passing panorama of trees and fields against the fading autumn sky. Adam had seen that the car headlights were already switched on, sending an everchanging pattern of shadow shapes across the road. Everything appeared wonderfully mysterious and exciting except for this niggling sense of responsibility spoiling things. 'I'm sure there'll be plenty of admirers wanting to dance with you,' she said, not meaning it. 'Anyway, the Wentworths'll see you're not neglected.'

'That's it. That's what I don't *want*. To be a *duty*.' Cassandra's head suddenly rose like that of a slender bird's from the blue velvet. For a moment she looked a different girl, alive and indignant.

Kate was surprised. 'Why, Cass–'

'Oh, leave me alone,' Cassandra slumped back. The quick interlude was over, and she was subdued again. Almost sullen.

Kate shrugged.

'If that's how you feel. Very well. But there's no need to look a martyr. I was thinking about you, that's all. Wanting us *both* to be happy. Not just me.'

Cassandra didn't reply.

A few minutes later the car slowed up to negotiate a sharp corner leading from the main road back to narrower lanes skirting the fringe of woodland country. Through the fitful light beads of perspiration glistened at the back of Adam's neck under his uniform cap. Kate saw his jaws clench determinedly as he jerked the gears. They were climbing a thread of hill between tall hedges that swayed ghost-like through the thin rising mist sending blurred shadow shapes across the road. There was a grinding sound and a momentary jerk as the Daimler came to a sudden halt then moved on again. Kate reached for the little speaking horn that led on a communication cord through the glass panel to the driver's seat.

'What was it? What was the matter?'

'A rabbit, miss, that's all,' Adam answered half turning his head to the horn. Then more loudly, 'Just a rabbit.'

Kate gave a sigh of relief and sank back. 'It could have been anything, or – *any*one,

31

couldn't it?' she remarked to Cassandra. 'Dreadful thought. But adventurous some-how.'

'I suppose so.'

'Oh, Cass, *do* cheer up. We shan't be long now. Charnbrook isn't far from the Monastery, and I saw that poking through the trees just now. They don't talk, you know – the monks. They're a silent brother-hood. Just fancy. Oh, I don't know how anyone could live like that – I suppose it's very worthy of them. But just imagine! – no fun or contact with other people. No romance. They must love God terribly.'

'If you can call it God.'

Kate made no further attempt at conversation. Cass really was the limit, she thought resentfully. After all the trouble taken over the dress and efforts spent to make her feel at ease and in a mood to enjoy Isabella's invitation she might at least *try* to be sociable. After all, she had been asked as a member of the Barrington family. Unless she cheered up and managed at least a smile Heaven alone knew what Jon Wentworth would think.

Rising indignation deepened the rose glow in Kate's cheeks, but when, a few minutes later the car turned down the drive to Charnbrook Hall, the fret of Cass was magically forgotten. Lights streamed from the open door down the terrace steps and, as the car drew to a halt, the sound of laughter and chatter and tinkle of music flooded the dusk. A footman was waiting to show the girls through the wide-open doors; Isabella was hovering about inside surrounded by a small group of young people in evening dress. She was looking quite stunning, Kate thought, in ivory satin, with something sparkling and fussy holding her pale shining hair in a shimmering roll on the top of her small head. The bodice of her dress was tightly waisted, cut *almost* but not quite as low on the shoulders as Kate's gown. She darted forward and greeted them effusively, while a maid in frilly black and white waited nearby to show them to the powder room.

Kate's memories of those first moments at Charnbrook remained in her mind always as a confused impression of soft perfumed air, the swish of silk, and soft chatter and laughter of youthful voices as elegantly clad feminine bodies pressed and peered at their reflected images through numerous mirrors. Heads turned and conversation momentarily lowered when Kate and Cassandra entered. Knowing her appearance would be spectacular among the softer muted shades of pinks, blues, lavenders and frilly whites, Kate lifted her head an inch higher; she could sense during the brief hush – curiosity, envy perhaps – or was it merely resentment stirring the little crowd? She was known, of course, to one or two, and probably the fact of her being Walter's daughter, and merely *Trade* made her a target for criticism. For a second she wondered if her mother had been right, and she should have worn something less daring?

Just as quickly the thought was dispelled. With a small sweet smile, she stepped forward followed by Cassandra and said in light, very clear tones, 'Pardon me, may I just have a *teeny* glimpse of myself in the mirror? I feel so very windblown.'

A rather plump girl, a stranger to Kate, moved away grudgingly with a faintly hostile glance, and sprayed herself liberally with cologne behind her ears.

Kate turned her head briefly. 'Come along, Cassandra, there's room for both of us.'

She stared at her reflection for a brief few seconds, turning her head critically from side to side on her slender neck. The image was reassuring. Her heart leaped. Cassie registered only as a fragile shadow at her shoulder.

Poor Cass, she thought with a wave of genuine sympathy. She really *would* do her best to see she wasn't entirely neglected. 'Put more perfume on,' she whispered, 'and don't look so *serious*. If you'd only *smile* a bit, Cass, it would make such a difference.' But Cassandra of course with her strict dreary upbringing wasn't *au fait* with scent or powder or the art of beguiling men. It really must be awful having such a boring background. Still, she, Kate, had done what she could on her cousin's behalf. The rest really was up to her, and with this consoling thought Kate let the matter drop.

Presently the two girls had joined a throng of guests in the large lounge, an ornate high-ceilinged room, brilliantly lit by crystal chandeliers hanging from the encrusted ceiling and on brackets round the walls. There was a tinkle of glass, the sound of corks popping, and excited murmurs and laughter of voices as black-coated male figures in evening dress merged with the froth of feminine frills, moving from group to group with glasses of champagne, or milder wines and fruit juices for any particular eye-catching girl of individual choice.

A footman was in charge of the buffet at one end of the long room, and a maid busy with silver trays of sandwiches.

The Hon. Jon soon noticed Kate and was quickly by her side staring down at her admiringly.

'I say!' he remarked, 'we do know each other, don't we? We last met at that old girl's garden party. I must say you look quite – ravishing.'

The hot blood mounted Kate's face.

She smiled. 'Thank you.'

He took her hand and pressed it. 'I shall have to see your card is filled before any other greedy bounder gets a chance.' His eyes briefly turned to Cassandra who was standing very upright and still a few inches in Kate's shadow.

'And this is–?' his voice wavered.

'Cassandra. A – a relative of mine – a kind of cousin.'

'Ah, yes. Isabella did tell me.'

The half-teasing, light-hearted quality had suddenly disappeared.

Bored already, Kate thought.

The next moment seemed to confirm it.

He was very polite, of course. He took Cass's white-gloved hand in his, and said in formal tones, 'I'm very pleased to meet you, Miss–?'

'Blacksley,' Kate said, not waiting for Cass herself to give the information. 'Cassandra Blacksley.'

He nodded. 'I'll try to remember. But if you'll forgive me for just a bit – I'll see you later – in the ballroom.'

He disengaged himself and zig-zagged

away into the crowd, leaving Kate with a rising sense of anger and disappointment. What she'd feared was already happening. Cassandra was spoiling everything.

The next half an hour was to register later as a mere blur in Kate's memory.

The orchestra, at the far end of the magnificent ballroom was already tuning up for a waltz when Kate and Cassandra entered accompanied by Bertie Foster, recently graduated from Oxford. He was the son of a lawyer and well acquainted with the Barrington family. Kate had felt relief when he'd appeared on the scene. Here, she'd thought, was someone able to take Cassie off her hands for a bit. He was good-natured, tall, fair, light-hearted, and interested in art more than the legal profession he was expected to follow. Just right for Cass.

'May I?' he said, indicating Kate's little dance card dangling from her wrist.

'Oh, but–' Kate paused. Only a few yards off she saw Jon's form making his way towards them. 'There's Cassie,' she reminded Bertie, 'we can't just–'

Her voice wavered speculatively, and during the following brief seconds Jon was there, smiling with an eager anticipatory look on his face.

Kate's heart fluttered. Her eyes were bright; the rose of her cheeks was emphasized by the brilliant light on her glossy curls. She had never looked lovelier. Unconsciously she took a short step towards him.

And then the shock came.

He gave her a brief nod, then by-passed her and moved straight to Cassandra who stared at him coolly for a moment, looking like some pale effigy of a character out of *A Midsummer Night's Dream,* while he indicated her dance card and, with something in his expression that shocked Kate, took it from the slim, outstretched white hand and started scribbling his name on it. Kate winced inwardly. Feeling outraged and hurt she looked round for Bertie, but he'd disappeared. Only one face in the nearby crowd was known to her – that of a dark, rather sardonic-looking man – Rick Ferris, standing just inside the door.

Her glance was held by his. Was it her fancy that his expression was faintly amused? She had a feeling he'd witnessed the little incident and sensed her humiliation. Anger replaced shock in her. She lifted her head proudly, wild colour flaming her cheeks, and turned away.

Strains of the 'Blue Danube' already floated sweetly, insidiously, through the air. One by one couples took to the floor. Kate noticed a somewhat florid middle-aged gentleman with a paunch approaching her. She moved hurriedly past a little group where an MC was busy about his duties. She was oblivious of anything but a wild desire to escape – to be alone somewhere – the powder room, where she could recover her equanimity, and avoid the further hurt of seeing insipid Cassandra being swirled around in Jon's arms.

Cassie! – that insignificant pale-faced little creature who hadn't a word to say for herself, and Jon – *Jon*.

How *could* he?

Half-blindly she pushed her way towards the door, and almost ran straight into the tall form of Rick Ferris.

She stopped, with a start, as he said, 'Miss Barrington! – not leaving yet, I hope. You're not faint surely? In that case, allow me–'

She pulled herself together abruptly.

'No, no. I'm quite all right. I just – I think I've left my handkerchief in the powder room–' She broke off knowing he did not believe her. There was a twinge of laughter at the corner of his lips, and his eyes had a shrewd disconcerting look as he stared at the tempestuous slender figure confronting him. The dip between her white breasts was faintly shadowed above the low-cut crimson bodice, the dark eyes luminous with the glitter of temper and unshed tears under disarranged curls of chestnut hair.

'I think you are mistaken,' he said, in quiet even tones. 'Isn't it poking out of your bag?'

She glanced down at the spangled pockette dangling from one wrist, with the card. He was right. The handkerchief was there.

'Oh how – how stupid of me–'

'But lucky for me. The moment I spotted you – looking so very striking, if I may say so

– among that bunch of frilly dollies – I decided you were the only one worth a second glance. I was about to cut across and grab my chance of a dance, when you bolted.'

There was a slight pause until he added, 'In the right direction luckily. So – may I have the pleasure, Miss Barrington?'

In a kind of daze Kate agreed, and a second or two later his arm was about her waist, and they were gliding across the polished floor in perfect rhythm as though they could have been practising for quite a time.

Once or twice, through the haze of figures and her own mixed emotions, she caught a glimpse of Cassie and Jon drifting by. She ignored them purposefully, her head high, smiling up into Rick's face. He was tall – quite the tallest man in the room. With his lean, strong features that were almost piratical they must appear the most spectacular couple on the floor. The knowledge raised her spirits. She'd show them; show them all – including Jon – that she, Kate Barrington, had sufficient feminine allure to captivate the man whom many women would consider a brilliant catch.

His background, though hardly aristocratic – his father had been a journalist, his mother, it was rumoured, on the stage, of Welsh extraction – could be ignored in the face of his other attributes, including his striking looks, the fact of his wealth, for he was very, very rich, and that at his age in the mid-thirties he had still evaded the matrimonial net. An aloof quality about him was tantalizing, though in business circles, and farming – he owned hundreds of acres of valuable land, and a stud bordering the forest – he was respected and well liked. He lived at Woodgate, a picturesque village only six miles from Lynchester, which enabled easy access to the thriving Midland town. As chief shareholder of the daily newspaper, the *Lynchester Times*, he journeyed there almost daily for meetings and to keep a personal eye on what was going on.

He could be generous to any charities he considered deserving, but critics resented what was termed the 'mean streak' in him, which seemed aware if even a penny stamp went missing according to the books of firms he had considerable interests in.

On the other hand his private life was frequently the scene of lively parties. It was known he had a 'lady friend' – a widow, a Mrs Linda Wade, who appeared periodically for the weekend at his home. 'Well – rather more than *friend*, my dear,' one thwarted ambitious mama had whispered significantly to another. 'She was on the *stage* you know. Like his mother. Blood will out.'

Such comments, however, had in no way deflected from the obvious advantages any future young woman would acquire in becoming Mrs Rick Ferris.

Kate had met him only once, briefly, since her return from France at a rose show organized by her father. With her mind already concentrated so romantically on the Hon. Jon, his presence had not registered, except as a somewhat arrogant individual who gave her the impression of owning the whole event. This hadn't been at all a fair assessment, of course. He'd done nothing obvious to impress his power on the public; in fact rather the reverse, by merely sauntering round, taking an interest in the exhibits without much socializing. But there was something about him – something difficult to explain – that seemed to place him as a man apart – different; a little irritating perhaps, but impossible completely to ignore.

And how fortunate, at this moment, Kate told herself, with her head whirling, that it should be so. Her dignity was restored with a surging through her of bitter-sweet pride as her body responded to the firm pressure and rhythmical movements of his. Triumph and a wild sense of abandonment possessed her. Her feet seemed to float on air. Like the wings and feathers of some gorgeous tropical bird the crimson silk gown billowed and swirled brilliantly through the crowd of dancers. Even when the strains of the orchestra died on a last quivering note, Kate and Rick were still moving.

Then, very slowly, his arm round her waist slackened into grudging release, and they stood for a moment, quite still, until her dizziness cleared.

He glanced down at her for a moment

before offering his arm and guiding her from the floor. She smiled at him with a contrived sweetness about her lips, aware of faces staring and doing her best to impress. Let them think what they like, she decided defiantly; she didn't care, or about Jon either.

Following three dances with Cassandra Jon approached her for a polka, which she declined coolly, saying she was sorry – she was otherwise engaged. Rick supported her, and Jon merely shrugged, then moved back sharply to Cassandra. With a faintly possessive gesture Ferris momentarily touched her waist.

'What a risk I took,' he said, 'in not filling your card earlier. If you hand it to me I'll amend the error immediately.'

He held out his hand and Kate automatically took it from her bag and gave it to him.

He glanced at it briefly and placed it in his pocket.

'Shall we take a breath of air?' he suggested. 'It's rather warm in here, don't you think?'

She agreed, and together they walked

conspicuously from the ballroom into the great hall, and from there through a lounge where a few elderly guests were gathered, with two or three couples who were not dancing. A glass partition led into a large conservatory which had further doors opening to the grounds outside.

A drift of heady perfume from exotic plants subtly intermingled with that of wines and scents of bodies and food hung insidiously in the warm air as Rick guided her through.

'Do you want to rest?' he said. 'Or take a stroll? But you haven't your shawl, have you. I'll go back for it–'

'No.' Her voice was emphatic. 'I'm used to fresh air. I love it. You needn't worry. I shan't be cold.'

With a shrewd yet enigmatic glance at the rich white and rose of her skin and dark eyes brilliant with excitement and glowing life, he had to agree.

'Very well. If the worst comes to the worst there is always my coat for your – bare shoulders.'

She flushed and placed her right hand

across the left breast letting her gloved fingers rest near her throat. A wave of unexpected self-consciousness swept through her.

'I suppose you think I look rather – gaudy,' she remarked childishly. 'My mother didn't approve of this red. *Or* the cut. But–' She swallowed and when he said nothing immediately she added quickly, 'I'm nearly nineteen you know. Old enough to know my own mind, I think.'

'Certainly.' He led her through the door into the sweet air of the gardens, saying, 'No need for explanations, Miss Barrington. If you must know, I approve your choice; you look quite magnificent.'

'No I don't. You're laughing at me. I – I wish you wouldn't. As a matter of fact–'

'As a matter of fact,' he interrupted, 'you're in the middle of an emotional crisis, I believe. It's the Honourable Jonathan, isn't it? – oh, don't worry. No one else would guess or have an inkling. But I have eyes in my head you know, and I'm a man of the world. I noticed your expression when he whirled away with your pale-faced little cousin. She is your cousin, isn't she?'

'A sort of adopted one. But it isn't really your business, is it? *Or* the dress. Or Jon. *Or* me.' She spoke haughtily to disguise her discomfort.

'No,' he agreed. 'Not yet.'

They were walking down a narrow path between hedges of some night-flowering shrub. The scent was overpowering, almost hypnotic. She stopped walking for a second.

'What do you mean, not yet?'

'Simply that I hope we can be friends in the future. Perhaps more. Who knows?'

She brushed a curl away from her cheek. 'It takes time to become friends – *real* friends, Mr Ferris.'

'Not for some people. I'm not the patient sort. Neither I'm sure are you. And for Heaven's sake, less of the "Mr Ferris". Rick's my name, short for Richard. And I'm damned if I'm going to go on calling you "Miss Barrington". Oh, don't worry' – he lifted a hand with a negative gesture – 'I'm not about to ravish or even kiss you, nothing familiar, although I've a shrewd idea some of the old girls – pardon me, *ladies* – in the lounge will be thinking so – that's inevitable, looking like you do, and me being what I am.'

She glanced at him speculatively, then remarked, feeling more at ease, 'You speak like some kind of brigand. Not the murderous kind, exactly, but rather wicked.'

'I can be, if the occasion warrants it. There are things I don't like which rile me. Seeing an attractive girl like you for instance, hurt by some conceited aristocratic young bounder like the Honourable Jon.'

She pulled her arm sharply from his.

'Don't.'

'Oh, I have to if we're to understand each other. I've been quite content for you to use me for the one evening, Kate, but after this any sharing basis wouldn't be my cup of tea. I hope that's clear.'

She shook her head.

'Nothing's clear tonight. I'm just – can't we talk about something else instead of *feelings*?'

He laughed. 'Of *course*. Choose the subject. I'll listen.'

She pulled herself together. 'It would be

nice to go for a walk – a *real* walk, but of course, it would be stupid, wouldn't it – dressed like this? I mean–'

'Slightly. We could share my coat, of course. But if you don't like tongue-wagging it would be better not. Come along now; we'd better get back. Take a good sniff of fresh air then we'll brave the crowd again.'

She stood for a moment, turned her head and stared into the soft damp dusk. 'I expect Beacon Hill's that way. You could see it I expect from the tump where the gazebo is.'

'Yes.'

'And your home is at Woodgate, quite near here. Near the Beacon, I mean. Ours is–'

'Why the geography lesson?'

She shrugged, and gave a short laugh. 'Oh, I don't know. I just – think we're very lucky to live round here.'

'There are more spectacular parts of the country.'

'But not like this. This is different, mysterious – secret somehow – perhaps because it's so old. Funny, isn't it, to think that all the rocky tumps of hills were once great volcanic mountains. Fancy! and right in the middle of England. They say it became King Lear's land. Did you know that?'

'My dear young lady! – enough of history. There's another waltz starting. Listen!' From within, above the confused murmur of movement and voices, the rhythmical sounds of Strauss beckoned. 'And I've a fancy to have my arm round your waist.'

His fancy took over almost immediately and minutes later when Kate had tidied her hair they were entering the ballroom.

The birthday event continued until two in the morning, and during the remaining hours Kate, for the sake of appearances, danced twice with Jon. It was quite clear to her that his thoughts were elsewhere; at moments his eyes strayed from her searching for – well, of course, for Cassandra – Kate told herself bitterly – pale, colourless Cassie who'd been invited to Charnbrook only from a sense of duty, and wearing *her* dress. *Hers.* Perhaps Kate's figure stiffened. Jon suddenly forced his attention upon her. 'It was jolly of you both to come,' he said with a slight inflection on the 'both', 'your cousin's a top-hole little dancer. I hear her mama has a dressmaking establishment.' Kate had a desire to scream *establishment?* – it's *nothing*. She helps her mother – her *adopted* mother – in a back room of a dreary house in a big dirty town, and that dress she's wearing is one of my cast-offs. Don't you remember – it was *me* you saw in it first?

But she kept the flow of words back. She must retain her dignity at all costs. And anyway there was no point in trying to carry on any conversation against a background of music and dancing.

She and Rick spent most of the remaining hours together, either dancing, relaxing in the conservatory, or at the buffet. Nearing the end of the evening, when she accidentally dropped one of her white velvet gloves, he picked it up and said, 'I will keep this as a memento,' and put it in his pocket.

But at the finale, when the bars of the last waltz faded, she felt she really knew him little better than at the beginning of the party.

Her father's Daimler was waiting in the drive below the front terrace steps, with Adam standing by to open the doors of the car for the two girls.

Ferris took Kate's hand and pressed it lightly before saying, 'Au revoir. Be good.' She didn't look at his face, just nodded, and with her cloak pulled to her chin hurried to the car. She glanced back impatiently for Cassie, and saw her at the top of the steps, just out of the door with Jon trying to retain her attention, obviously whispering some endearment. Rick had disappeared. Cassandra tore herself away, and a minute later was seated by Kate on the lush back seat of the car while Adam cranked the engine.

Presently they were moving through the gates of the grounds and had turned past the lodge into the lane towards the main road.

Adam drove cautiously, never motoring above twenty miles an hour which was considered by most people quite fast for such a large car, especially at night.

Nothing to Kate seemed quite real any more. The rocky tumps of Burnwood Hills emerged fitfully against the landscape of trees and misted moonlight as they passed down the thread of roadway. The excitement and tension of the evening had left her exhausted emotionally, and it didn't help matters when Cassandra said softly, 'He's nice, isn't he?'

'Who?' Crossly, although she knew.

'Jon.'

'He's all right. I told you you'd be looked after. The Wentworths know how to behave.'

'He didn't make me *feel* only like that though.'

Kate's head gave a jerk round. She hadn't *meant* to look at Cassie; she didn't want to. But something in the quiet voice, a certain smug sweetness, was too much for her.

Cassandra was staring ahead as though hypnotized, spell-bound, by some image or memory withheld from Kate. In the changing play of shadows reflected through the windows, of course, it was impossible actually to *see* her expression, but the stillness of the slim form swallowed in the blue velvet – the confident assertion and atmosphere only emphasized Kate's conviction that Cassandra had somehow managed to inveigle herself into Jon's affection and esteem. And it was ridiculous; she had no looks, no background, nothing at all in keeping with the Wentworth's world. How had she managed it? Pity, perhaps, and a certain slyness that had played up to a sympathetic strain in Jon's nature.

It must be that. Yes, Cassie had been sly. A real sly puss.

In spite of her tiredness Kate had a sudden desire to slap her cousin sharply across the cool pale cheek conveniently next to her.

But she again restrained herself.

One didn't, after all, resort to vulgar brawls in a Daimler in the early hours of the morning. All the same – I detest her, she thought in a rising wave of anger. Yes, I do.

As quickly as it had flared up, the hot wave of temper died, and she was momentarily ashamed. Jon had a right to dance with whom he liked; that he had chosen Cass instead of herself proved she lacked something the other girl had.

Or was it the red dress? *Had* it been wrong, as her mother had suggested?

Sitting miserably silent for the rest of the journey back to Beechlands she knew she'd never wear it again. She'd give it away; one of the maids could have it, or perhaps, ironically, Cassie. It had been an expensive dress to buy. Such a gift could absolve her from any guilt on her part for having felt such violent animosity against her cousin.

Cassie hadn't been aware of it anyway, she told herself defensively. In her quiet way she was far too concerned with her own feelings to think of anyone else.

It was past three before the girls got to bed, and another hour passed before Kate managed to sleep. Yet she woke at her usual early hour, dressed and went for a walk before breakfast in an effort to get her memories of the evening's events into perspective. A dull ache of disappointment and sense of betrayal filled her. How could Jon have acted as he had? *How?* And why? And with Cassie of all people, dull colourless Cassandra? Even if the red dress *had* been a mistake if he'd possessed a shred of feeling he wouldn't have allowed it to spoil what had promised to be friendship between them. Maybe she shouldn't have flaunted herself quite so blatantly with Rick

Ferris, or have refused to dance with him the first time he'd asked her, following his early choice of Cass. But she'd had to show him that Kate Barrington had no intention of being treated as second best.

Oh, well! – there'd be other times. Surely there would be. Her spirits lifted a little. Cassie would be gone in a fortnight anyway.

But, as things turned out, Cassie wasn't. After Kate returned from her walk that day a letter came from Cassie's mother urging her to stay a little longer at Beechlands, and this was agreed.

The autumn was a golden one that year, and comparatively mild. Never had the forest area looked more beautiful.

In the early mornings the trees emerged orange and brown through thin veils of silvered mist, and the tip of Beacon Hill shone bright in the rising sunlight beyond Woodgate where Rick Ferris had his home. Occasionally Kate rode her mare, Beth, in that direction and cantered up the slope to the summit. The atmosphere never failed to stir her imagination and senses. There, in the far past, prehistoric man had built earthworks, and millions of years before that the range of Burnwood Hills had erupted and risen as great volcanic mountains. In the centuries of recent times religious orders had thrived in peace and built sanctuaries. Travellers of Romany blood in bright caravans still wended their ways through shadowed secret lanes leading from Larchborough to Lynchester, tethering their horses and making camp *en route* before joining fairs or doing business in the towns selling brooms and posies from door to door.

During the days immediately following Cassandra's decision to spend a further indefinite period at Beechlands, Kate acquired a regular habit of riding Woodgate way, hoping she might encounter Ferris – not because she felt consciously attracted, but to captivate once again and retain the balm he'd given her hurt pride at Isabella's dance. She had an uneasy feeling that Cassie and Jon had made some kind of pact to meet again, and the thought not only hurt but irritated her, making her increasingly restless and anxious for an outlet to her repressed emotions. Kate was unlucky, however, in any idea she had at that time of a chance encounter with Ferris. Being an astute business man embroiled, among other things, in producing a new newspaper, *The Lynchester Monitor*, he was off in the early hours to the town, and frequently did not return to Woodgate until a late hour, or perhaps not at all when he took the train to London for some meeting or other with business colleagues or rivals.

So Kate was left frustrated and bitter, pondering again on the annoying situation concerning Cassandra and Jon.

The growing rift between the two girls had widened, though neither spoke of it. Kate was too proud to enquire where Cassie was going when she set off with her pad and paint-box, presumably for a session of sketching, or to suggest accompanying her. She had never done so in the past, and it would be *too* humiliating to show curiosity now. She didn't think much of Cassie's delicate watercolours anyway. All the same, there was a difference in Cass these days, not only in looks which had a kind of ethereal secretive quality about them that was tantalizing, but in behaviour.

Before the occasion of the dance the timetable of her days had been fairly predictable; she'd either spend the mornings wandering about the expansive Beechlands gardens making pencil sketches of flowers and wildlife, or take a certain ramble to the nearby copse, returning early for lunch, then, in the afternoon mooning – Kate's expression – in the library with a book. Occasionally they went together with Emily on a shopping expedition to Lynchester. Now her routine had changed; in fact there was no definite routine at all. One moment Cass would be in the conservatory perhaps, or arranging flowers in the lounge, the next she'd have slipped off, and if wanted casually for some reason, was nowhere to be found.

And her disappearances were so quietly and effectively contrived that Kate was disturbed, suspecting the reason.

'I think she's meeting someone,' she said to her mother one day, when her cousin couldn't be located. 'Haven't you noticed how – odd – she's been lately? Always slinking off by herself, and sort of – well, self-satisfied.'

Emily laughed the question off. 'My dear girl, Cassandra's always been the quiet sort. She likes her own company, especially when she's got immersed in some idea for a new painting–'

'Pooh! I don't believe it's a painting at all.'

Emily looked mildly surprised. 'It's not like you to be so bothered about Cassie,' she remarked quietly. 'Why is it Kate?'

Recovering herself, Kate answered, 'Oh, nothing really. Yes, I suppose you're right. It was just – well, there are gypsies about. You wouldn't want her getting entangled with any of those, would you?'

But it wasn't gypsies she was thinking of, it was Jon.

'No, I wouldn't, and I'm certainly not at all bothered about such a thing,' Emily replied firmly. 'I'm quite sure Cassandra has far more sense.'

'Forget it then,' Kate remarked, trying to sound practical. 'I'm probably imagining things.'

'I'm sure you are.'

But however easy it was to close the subject with words, facts suggested otherwise when two days later Cassandra confided to Kate that Jon had invited her to Charnbrook for the afternoon and tea following, if her aunt, Mrs Barrington, agreed.

The words came out in a soft flurry of excitement, there was a tinge of colour in her usually delicately pale cheeks.

'I – I was painting at a place near Feyland,' she said, 'it's lovely there. I often go, and Jon – happened to turn up. He said it would be all right if you came too. His mother has some watercolour sketches that are very old – her grandmother did them, and she thought–'

'Oh, you needn't explain,' Kate interrupted sharply, as a rush of jealous anger rose in her. '*You* go. I'm not interested in art like you are, and tea-talk bores me anyway.'

'You don't *mind*, do you? He'll collect me – in his car, I think, and bring me back. Will Aunt Emily agree?'

'You'd better ask her,' Kate said, 'but I'm sure she'll be delighted for you to have any – *proper* – social connection with the Wentworths. It's quite an achievement, you know.'

Instantly she regretted the sarcasm – the touch of bitterness. To be *jealous* of *Cassie* was somehow degrading. So she forced herself to smile and added more casually, 'It will be nice for you. And Mama will be pleased, I know she will. Only I just wish you'd said something to me before about meeting Jon. You must have been seeing him: I often wondered.'

She was staring very directly into the other girl's face.

Cassandra looked away. 'Only once – twice with this last time. There was nothing secret about it. Not really. We just happened to like the same sort of things and places. It's a kind of ruin near Feyland. I've been sketching it. I'll show you, if you like.'

Kate's irritation returned. 'Oh, don't bother. It's not important. You've done so many. If Jon appreciates your creations, that's all that matters, isn't it?'

64

Cassie's luminous eyes widened. Her soft voice had a cool condemning quality when she said, 'I believe you're annoyed.'

'Don't be stupid.' Kate turned away. 'I'm going for a canter on Beth. You'd better get Mama to suggest what you wear for your assignment at the Wentworths. Tell her I've given you the pick of my wardrobe —all except the jade. That's not worn yet.'

It was in such a mood of defiant bravado that five minutes later Kate, riding towards Woodgate, met Rick Ferris cantering leisurely round a bend of woodland fringing the village.

He drew up, reined, and she did the same, smiling.

'Good morning, Kate. Nice day, isn't it?' His teeth were a flash of white in the sunlight. He wore no hat and with the soft wind ruffling his dark hair looked younger than she remembered in formal attire.

'Yes, lovely,' she agreed.

'Looking for me, were you?' The teasing quality of his voice, the hint of mischief, brought a flash of embarrassment to her cheeks.

'Of course not. I don't go looking for men, Mr Ferris.'

He laughed. 'Forgive me. Of course you don't. You don't need to. You're far too beautiful.'

'This is a stupid conversation. I must be going. I only – ' She was about to kick Beth to a canter when he halted her.

'No, please. Allow me to accompany you, or let us get things fixed.'

She stared. 'What *do* you mean?'

'Our next rendezvous.'

'But, Mr Ferris—'

'Rick. Remember?'

Suddenly she realized there was no point in fencing. She *wanted* to see him again, not casually, or in a crowd, but at a properly arranged date which could restore her lost self-confidence and vanity that had been so wounded by Jon's conduct.

So it was arranged for her to visit the manor farm on an afternoon of the following week, when he would show her round the stud, before escorting her to Woodgate for a light evening meal.

'No frills or fuss,' he said, 'and you need

have no fear of offending the proprieties. All will be perfectly respectable. My house-keeper will be in charge. I shall have a word first with your papa, of course. So you can assure your mama I'm no wolf in sheep's clothing.'

In this way Kate Barrington's association with Rick Ferris continued towards a course of deepening intimacy.

During the weeks following, she told herself repeatedly she certainly did not love him, nor ever could. Always she'd long for Jon. But Rick was an exciting man to be with. And when he was not immersed in business matters he was fun, and he'd the capacity to make her laugh and enjoy life.

In late October when Cassie, who was still at Beechlands, stunned the Barringtons with the information that the Hon. Jon Wentworth had asked her to marry him and she'd agreed. Kate, inwardly outraged and shocked almost beyond belief, determined desperately to steal what social publicity she could from Cassandra's forthcoming union in being the first to wed.

By then she knew Ferris wanted her, and

was aware that he could have her only by making her his wife. She possessed all the subtle instincts of bringing him to the point. They were both intrinsically impatient, sensual people, and their engagement could be brief. He might not have the romantic allure of Jon, and she would never now be the future Lady Wentworth, but Rick Ferris mattered. She would be envied by many women and life would be an adventure. With tact and a little flattery from her he could be persuaded to give her whatever she wished – materially. Of that she was convinced. And in time, when Jon grew bored with colourless Cassandra, he'd notice his mistake.

That would be her ultimate triumph.

And so, reckless from reaction she plunged headlong into a new – and as it proved later – wildly disturbing relationship.

Kate's single-minded determination allied to Rick's increasing desire for her, brought her wish to fulfilment, and in November amid a lightning blaze of publicity she became the bride of Richard Ferris. Cassandra and the Hon. Jon Wentworth were among the guests present at the ceremony and reception.

The marriage of Sir William Wentworth's son to Cassandra Blacksley took place in February of the following year at the family's private chapel on the Charnbrook estate. Sir William Wentworth and his wife, Lady Olivia, who held the title in her own right being the youngest daughter of a duke, had grudgingly agreed to the union in the face of their son's stubborn infatuation and determination to take off to foreign climes if any means was produced to thwart him. And, after all, as Sir William pointed out, she would not be without a dowry. Barrington had come up trumps in that direction, and the girl seemed a quiet little thing – malleable. Jonathan might have done worse.

'That's true,' his wife had agreed thoughtfully. 'Yes, we must be thankful, I suppose, the dear boy didn't choose Barrington's showy daughter. I can see trouble ahead for Ferris. Mark my words – there's a wild streak in her. But, of course, he's no gentleman. They're well matched in that way. Bourgeois. You could see that at the wedding – all those bridesmaids, and champagne – *really*!'

'A good-looking filly, nevertheless,' Wentworth observed retrospectively. 'A fine figure too – tiny waist and good hips. Should breed well.'

'William! I believe you admire her.'

'Hm! She's got style whatever you may say, m'dear. But there now. Ferris and his bride are nothing to do with us. We've our own son to think of.'

'Indeed yes. And no vulgar publicity at the ceremony. The number of guests must be kept to a strict minimum. No outsiders at the service, just relatives and staff. Thank heaven for our private chapel. It would be quite odious to provoke any sense of rivalry in the press between the Wentworth and Barrington families.'

'There can be no question of that, Olivia,' William remarked drily, 'financially speaking. As you well know.'

'I was referring to class, William. Most wealthy people nowadays are of the lower social orders. Unfortunately.'

One of her husband's bushy eyebrows raised itself quizzically, 'Not for *them*, my dear. I've no doubt Ferris's millions are already adding more than a touch of spice to his saucy young wife's experience.'

At that moment, to be precise, Rick Ferris was watching Kate with considerable satisfaction and mounting desire, prepare herself before her mirror for what was likely to prove a somewhat tricky social occasion – dinner with John Monksley, a newspaper tycoon, and the much whispered about widow, Mrs Linda Wade, who had made herself notorious in the district through her visits to Woodgate, the Ferris home. It was early December, and Rick and Kate had only returned the previous week from their honeymoon in London and the Continent.

Kate's first instinct had been to object. But a gleam in her husband's eye – a certain wary challenge, had restrained her. Everything between the couple so far had been so amicable and pleasantly exciting, the wedding at Lynchester Cathedral a public triumph, to cause an unnecessary jarring note would be foolish on her part, and quite ineffectual, for she had already sensed in the short time of her marriage that when Rick Ferris set his mind to a thing he somehow carried it through.

'I want you to be pleasant to Mrs Wade,' he said. 'She has valuable contacts in London and abroad. Her experience theatrically, and with the Press is considerable. And I'm thinking of launching a monthly *Pictorial Gazette* dealing specifically with social matters, also with stage and cinema gossip. Picture houses are starting up. Already a film theatre has been built in Pittsburg. In another decade no city in this country will be without one – and I mean to be in a good thing at the very beginning. So – just be your most charming self tonight, will you?' A finger touched the back of her bare neck seductively, and from there travelled down the course of one white shoulder to a breast dislodging the flimsy wrap so it fell to her waist revealing a froth of underwear. She turned her head smiling up at him. 'Oh, Rick! *really*. Of course I will.'

He nodded, paused a moment staring at her reflectively, then gave a little jerk to the loosening of her corsets. 'That's my girl. My own sweet wife.'

A moment later she was lying supine and lovely beneath him on the bed, her luxurious hair spilling its cloud over the silk pillow, forgetful of everything in that brief sensuous interlude – even Jon, although when all was over it was still Jon she thought of, with a sense of shame, and romantic longing.

She felt confused and faintly condemning.

Rick was so *practical*. So somehow self-assured, accepting, even demanding, everything as *his* right.

The way he stood at that moment before the mirror – *her* mirror – regarding his countenance while feeling the line of his strong jaw and recently shadowed chin, his complacency as he jerked the cord of his silk wrap tightly above the athletic hips, the hips of a horseman, irritated her.

It was not himself he should be thinking of, but still *her*, so recently ravished.

Slightly deflated, she swung her long legs

out of the bed.

'When you've finished, darling,' she said, 'would you mind sparing an inch or two of the mirror? We have guests coming. Remember?'

He turned quickly to glance at her, a quirk of amusement about his lips.

'Sorry, madam. My pleasure.'

He stepped aside and pushed the chair into its place; she adjusted her underwear, tied the frilled petticoat at her waist and, before seating herself, said 'Do you mind pulling this lacing up, Rick. I really haven't got time to fiddle now. Your – guests are due to arrive in less than an hour, and there are certain things downstairs I have to attend to.'

'Of course. But I think you'll agree our little diversion was worth it.'

She didn't reply. Little diversion. How trivial a phrase to use. And yet how apt, how characteristic somehow of this worldly man she had married. And how little she really knew of him. Was that, for instance, indicative of his attitude to women in general? In particular to his former mistress

– if what rumour said was true – the widow, Mrs Wade, who she was due to entertain that evening?

A mounting sense of rivalry quickened in her, a spurt of temper which she controlled with an effort. Rick must never know she felt a shred of resentment towards any former amour of his. To do so would be undignified, and place her at an unpleasant disadvantage emotionally.

However, following the fleeting confusion of doubts, the trivialities of final preparations and mounting tension heralding the enforced meeting ahead, the event itself once under way, went more easily than Kate had anticipated.

The dinner itself was excellently prepared, and served, at the long mahogany table glinting with glass and silver under crystal chandeliers, with Rick at the head and his wife facing him from the opposite end. The guests sat on either side, and Kate noticed with satisfaction that Linda Wade's cheeks shone slightly damp despite her liberal coating of rouge. Probably she had a poor skin beneath the make-up. Her shoulders and arms were too plump for her dimpled small hands, and her fair fussed hair was far too yellow to be natural. Nevertheless her eyes were very blue and must once have been striking. Now they were small, peering from tiny networked wrinkles. But wary – oh, yes. They were shrewd watchful eyes, Kate decided. Was she jealous? The thought was stimulating and gave power to her performance as hostess. Her innate ability to put on an act pushed all other considerations aside; she became graciousness personified, listening attentively to any remark made by the other woman – with just a suggestion of an encouraging half-smile on her tilted mouth. What hidden rivalry there might be between the two was admirably concealed, except perhaps to Rick whose eyes at intervals glanced at Kate enigmatically, but with a whimsical knowledge that didn't escape her.

Still, on the whole, the evening was a success; outer politeness was never allowed to flag, even when the two men had retired to the smoking-room for a discussion of male topics and a brief business interval, leaving the women, following a session of adjusting their toilet, to get to know each other – Rick's phrase – in the drawing-room.

'My dear!' Linda said. 'I'm so *delighted* at having the opportunity to meet my old friend's new wife in her home at such an early date following the marriage. Most women envy you, of course, but at the wedding when I saw you looking so beautiful I almost envied Rick.' She paused, then continued with a touch of acid ambiguity, 'Not *entirely*, of course. Marriage is such a lottery, is it not? And, of course, you *are* very young. And Rick – well, naturally he's already had quite a deal of experience in life – which makes him a connoisseur in his way–'

'Of what, Mrs Wade?' Kate interrupted pertly. 'Are you referring to women?'

'Good gracious, darling! What a question. As if I'd dream of sticking my neck out in such a way. I was thinking of values.'

'I see.'

'Of people, and things. You'll have such a lot to discover – about matters in his life that are tremendously important to him.'

'I'm aware of that.'

'Oh, yes. I can well believe it,' Linda said drily. 'I'm sure you're a very intelligent young woman.'

Not quite knowing whether this observation was meant to be complimentary or otherwise, Kate changed the conversation into more impersonal channels, including theatrical gossip and plays currently being performed in London.

'I understand you were once – an actress yourself, Mrs Wade?' Kate ventured to ask at what she considered a tactful point.

Linda's eyes narrowed slightly; her voice was brittle bright, when she answered, 'You understand perfectly correctly, my dear. I certainly was. But then' – there was a short pause before she continued – 'we women are all actresses at heart, are we not? Which is why we contrive so cleverly to enchant our men.'

Kate's tell-tale flush tinged her cheeks. She forced a little laugh and answered, 'When we need to, I suppose, but thank goodness it isn't always necessary.'

'In youth, no. But as the years pass, believe me, when the first glamour of beauty is fading a clever brain is generally required to keep a certain type of man faithful.'

'By a certain type of man you mean men like my husband, Mrs Wade?' Kate retorted boldly. 'Oh, I'm certainly not bothered about such problems at the moment. Please don't worry about *my* future. Rick and I understand each other. And now' – with acid sweetness – 'your cup is empty. Will you have more coffee?'

'Thank you.'

A highly charged frisson of anger seemed to emanate from the plump figure through the atmosphere. Kate sensed that for the moment, anyway, she had won in the subtle battle of feminine jealousies.

It was only later, when the guests had departed, and Kate was alone in the bedroom before Rick joined her, that her encounter with Mrs Wade fully registered. Obviously whether Linda's former relationship with Ferris had been merely one of intimate friendship or something more serious, the ex-actress had no intention of abandoning what influence she still might have.

And from that moment Kate was fiercely resentful. Rick's life was hers now. *She* was mistress of Woodgate House, and did not intend to allow any other woman to have a say in their mutual existence. She might not love Rick, but he excited and fulfilled her, and one day, who knew? If he went into politics or was sufficiently successful in the number of newspapers and business ventures he had interests in, he might receive a knighthood. Then she would become Lady Ferris, and enjoy the triumph of facing Jon on an equal footing.

The picture acted like strong wine in her blood. Her eyes shone bright through the dark lashes, her cheeks had a rich peach glow from the rose-shaded lamplight. When Rick entered minutes later he was amazed once more, almost shocked by her beauty, and wonder stirred in him that she could really be his. This was an emotion he had so far managed to hide. Women, he'd found, in his thirty-six years, were contradictory creatures, and could be capricious if allowed to become too sure of a man.

So that evening was like so many others of lovemaking with his young wife, holding no expression of ardour in words – merely a deep sensuous coming together that left them at last at peace, though fleeting half-formed memories of Jon merged in Kate's mind, fading eventually into sleep.

2

The first discordant note in the Ferris household occurred when Kate expressed a dislike of attending the Wentworth wedding.

'It would really be so *embarrassing*,' she told her husband. 'With Aunt Blacksley being there – so drab and – and looking just what she is–'

'The mother of the bride,' Rick interrupted with what his wife should have detected as a dangerous edge to his voice.

'By adoption,' came the sharp correction. 'No one knows who Cassie's real mother was. And anyway the Wentworths are high church. Aunt Blacksley wouldn't know how to act. Her husband was *Methodist*. A minister. There's always ill-feeling between Free Church and anything veering towards Catholicism. And–'

Rick sighed. 'For Heaven's sake, Kate, be reasonable. We're talking of a wedding ceremony that should unite the Barringtons with the Wentworths. And Mrs Blacksley is all the family Cassandra has.'

'It isn't only that – the religious difference,' Kate persisted stubbornly. 'It's the church – that tiny chapel place. You know how I get claustrophobia in small places, and–'

Rick's eyebrows shot up. 'I know nothing of the sort. It's the first I've heard of it.'

'Well I do. I'd feel stifled and miserable, and there'll probably be an incense smell. That always makes me feel sick, and I know it would be better for Cass if I wasn't there.'

'Now, my love, you're being quite ridiculous. It's settled. We're going. To refuse would be downright rude and it's important to me to be thought well of in the district. So forget your doubts and qualms. Be a good girl and settle for something suitable and charming to wear, and look forward to the champagne and confetti and a happy day instead of glooming about having to take second place for once.'

Kate's eyes widened. She stared at him astonished. He had an expression on his face she'd never seen before – searching, almost grim as though for the first time he was reaching her most secret thoughts.

'What do you mean? Second place?' she asked, catching her breath slightly.

'I'm sure I don't have to explain; your own fancy for the Honourable Jon was clear enough at the time, if you remember. But that's an episode we should both do well to forget. So no more arguing about the wedding. We're *going*, that's that.'

He's insufferable, Kate thought, quite insufferable. But she said no more. Her fingers were clenched tightly over her handkerchief, rolling it into a small ball, and her jaws were set.

He'd won this time. In future, she determined, she'd have to be more subtle and play her part differently should any conflicting discussion arise between them.

It was the very first time she'd realized that marriage to Rick Ferris was not going to be all plain sailing.

Still, she'd been born a Barrington, and Barringtons generally succeeded in winning any challenge that arose. Her self-confidence gradually returned, and in the end her natural high spirits were revived by the contemplation of acquiring some eye-catching outfit that would evoke envy and admiration from the select congregation gathered to see the Honourable Jonathan Wentworth marry her cousin. She chose pale lavender silk for the occasion that accentuated her exquisite complexion, emphasizing the rich russet shades of her hair.

So, despite the brief dispute life assumed its original harmonious course at Woodgate, though Rick realized full well there might be occasional difficulties ahead.

It was in late January, the period shortly before the wedding that during one of Kate's canters on Beth through the winding forest lanes, that she came upon Cassie leaning against a tree, with her sketching pad under her arm. She was wearing a loose blue cape, and the wind had blown pale strands of fair hair over her shoulders. She appeared absorbed, staring at a glitter of light through a tangle of branches shielding a darker mass of something beyond, to her left.

For the first time Kate, with a lurch of astonishment, recognized that Cassandra in these surroundings had a certain beauty – a fey-like delicacy of form – a grace akin to that of a young deer and other of the forest creatures. She had never really fitted in at Beechlands, and its social life, but here, somehow, she appeared so right. Had Jon recognized this subtle quality? Was there something similar in the two of them that had so instantly captured his imagination? Or was it just happiness that had caused the change in a rather colourless young girl to gentle loveliness? If so, then it was wrong of her, Kate to grudge her the new status of becoming Jon's wife. She must be generous, she decided, and forgive her for stealing the man whom she'd so wanted for herself.

After all, nothing could make any difference now. In the space of two weeks they would *both* be married women – Mrs Rick Ferris, and the Hon. Mrs Jon Wentworth.

They must be friends – not only for Cassie's sake, but because she knew Rick wished it.

Cassandra turned as Kate reined and tethered her mount to the stump of a tree at the side of the lane. Then she pushed through the undergrowth and approached her cousin.

Cassandra gave a little start, as though she'd been woken sharply from a dream.

'So I've found you,' Kate remarked ineffectually. 'This is your secret place!'

'Secret? Well, it's where I like to come for ideas and things. For my paintings. There'll be orchids later, as well as bluebells wild, of course, but rare. Jon gave me a little book about them—' she broke off vaguely. Something in Kate's face – the way she stood, so completely still for a moment – a static shape against the pale light behind her was mildly disturbing to Cass.

'Ah, yes. Jon. I've heard he's a bit of a naturalist.'

'He is. We like the same things,' Cassandra stated with a sudden unexpected show of spirit. 'And this place isn't secret – anyone can come here, you know that. Or didn't you know—?' She turned, indicating the half-tumbled shape over the lane of a ruined cottage entangled in briars, elderberry and thorn, fifty yards or so away. 'That was once part of a priory, then something tragic happened. Later an old woman lived there who had strange powers, and she–'

'Oh, I know. I *know*,' Kate interrupted impatiently. 'There are lots of stories and legends about this district, but they shouldn't be taken as fact. True history's often a very different matter.'

'Yes. I suppose so.'

'Anyway – have you been sketching it?'

'Not today. Just thinking.'

'About the wedding?'

'Partly. You and Rick *are* coming, aren't you?'

'Naturally. But I don't suppose we shall stay long at the reception. There's going to be one, I suppose?'

'Just for relations – that's what Jon said, and the servants.'

'And Aunt Blacksley, of course, with my parents?'

Cassandra sighed. 'Why are you asking all these questions, Kate? You must have seen the invitation, or haven't you?'

Kate shrugged. 'Oh, I just glanced. But I do find celebrations – of *any* kind – rather boring. Of course' – she tried to simulate interest and warmth into her voice – 'it'll be different with *you*, Cass – being my – sort of cousin. And getting married too – to Jon.'

Cass smiled, and the smile gave her sudden radiance. 'Yes. And if it hadn't been for you, and that wonderful dance we'd probably never have met at all.'

No, Kate thought, with a sudden desperate feeling of loss and anger, you wouldn't. I was an idiot ever to agree taking you to that wretched birthday ball. It was Isobel's fault – I'll never forgive her, or you for the secret way you acted in stealing Jon.

Through this unexpected fresh spurt of jealousy it didn't occur to her that she herself had known Jonathan so very slightly, in fact hardly at all. Her expression had suddenly become hard and cold. But Cassandra didn't notice.

The tracery of dancing shadows from the trees dimmed bitterness into a mere blue of a face under a shining mane of russet hair.

'Would you like to see my latest

paintings?' Kate heard Cassandra saying in her light voice.

'Where are they?'

'Over there – in that little place – the ruin. I've sort of made it into a kind of studio. Jon helped me, of course. We call it the Tree Studio, because it's half made of branches now, and there's a beech tree at the back.'

Kate agreed automatically, and together they made their way across the path to the green thicket enclosing the tumbled building.

From the first it appeared to be no more than an overgrown tumbled hovel – a retreat for a wandering tramp perhaps and wild creatures seeking refuge from the elements. But a ray of light zig-zagged from inside, and when they'd pushed through the opening that had probably once been a door, a stream of early sunshine from a gothic-shaped window at the far end revealed an interior with a boarded floor – obviously recently installed – granite walls partially mended that had been thatched and were enclosed on the outside by the groping branches of sycamores and the spreading arms of the old beech tree. The remains of a fireplace were clearly in a state of being restored, and the holes in one rough wall were already filled in. A large tin of household paint stood in a corner facing a wooden bench and a cane chair. There was an oil stove and a stack of Cassandra's paintings pushed into an alcove.

'It will be quite different when it's finished,' Kate, in a daze, heard Cass saying. 'There's going to be a proper door, and that old stove won't be here, because Jon says oil is dangerous. He doesn't *really* like me coming alone here yet. I'm supposed to bring the dog with me anyway. But I just had a sudden longing, somehow, to be here quite alone for once. Funny, isn't it, that you should appear? But I'm glad now, because I wanted you to know.'

'*Why?*' Kate's voice was sharp.

'Well, we're cousins, aren't we? Oh, I know you're not really interested in painting – not mine anyway. But we've done things together, and if ever you want to share it you can.'

'As I don't paint there wouldn't be much

point, would there? Still, I'm glad you've got your own retreat at last.'

'Jon doesn't call it that,' Cassandra said with a shy half-smile. 'Our Tree Studio – that's what he's named it.'

'Quite apt,' Kate remarked shortly. She felt Cassandra's eyes on her questioningly, and wondered if she'd sensed – even slightly – the sudden sharp pain she felt – the quite irrational envy, because after all she was Mrs Ferris now – of picturing Jon making love to Cassie in that romantic, somehow unreal, setting.

'Isn't it rather a long way from Charnbrook to have a studio?' she asked mechanically.

'That won't matter. And it's not so far if you take the shortest cut. Anyhow, I'm learning to ride now, side saddle of course – I've a mare of my own in the stable at Charnbrook; and there's always my bicycle.'

'*You?* On a horse? But you never used to like them. They frightened you.'

'This one's different. Gentle, not much more than a foal – and quite white. Her name's Snowfire.'

Snowfire! Snowfire? the word echoed through Kate's brain tormentingly. And a gift from Jon. The picture evoked a fairytale quality about it of Cassandra riding through the forest like some legendary princess on a white palfrey to meet her lover.

Yet her voice was calm when she said, 'You're lucky, Cass. I hope you'll be happy.'

And in a way this was true. Bitterness had died in Kate as quickly as it had flamed up; there was no point in fretting for something that never, now, could be hers. In any case she wasn't the fairytale type. But then, was Jon?

Brushing the question aside, she said abruptly, 'I must get back. Rick's returning from a London visit this morning, he may already be back at Woodgate. I want to be there when he arrives.'

'But can't you just have a proper look at my paintings?'

'Another time. I know about your hide-out now.'

Minutes later she was cantering back towards the village. She was unaware of the unshed tears brimming to her eyes until the brushes of cool wind whipped their dampness to her cheeks. One hand rubbed them quickly away. Her lower lip tightened with resolve, and when she reached the red-brick mansion of her home her smile was brilliant as Rick came to meet her. His kiss was firm and warm on her mouth. She closed her eyes, briefly willing herself to forgetfulness through the dark tide of his rising passion.

'I've missed you,' she replied.

It was true. Only through him could she dispel the longing sense of loss – and of an emotion to which she could give no name.

The wedding at Charnbrook passed quietly as the Wentworths had intended it should, with only a small crowd of onlookers at the gates of the estate, to watch the comparatively small number of cars and guest carriages drive through to the family chapel.

As Rick and Kate passed in their carriage and pair, Kate was aware of faces peering admiringly from the sides of the lane. She knew she looked ravishing, and the knowledge combined with Rick's pride in her added to her self-confidence and beauty.

Cassandra, to the contrary, appeared a shy and rather fragile bride as she walked up the aisle for the ceremony on her uncle's – William Barrington's – arm. Kate wondered once or twice during the ceremony what Jon could ever have seen in her. During their brief accidental meeting at the Tree Studio she had almost understood; amongst the mysterious shadowed background of the forest Cassie had possessed an elusive, almost elfin, quality – the background of trees and undergrowth had suited her. But the conventional white bridal dress had dimmed what character she possessed into a mere representation of any ordinary girl dressed up for the occasion – colourless, and rather dull; the Cassie Kate had known through the years.

Rick, however, thought differently. In the bedroom after their return home following the reception, he said, 'Cassandra came up to scratch, didn't she? No fumbling for words or unintelligible "I do". An attractive little thing too, in her way.'

'You think so?' Kate said shortly. 'Oh, I suppose so. I don't think the white suited her though. If I'd been Cassie I'd have chosen peach, it would have given her more colour.'

'Ah, but you're not Cassie,' Rick said lightly, giving her an overt glance. 'Thank God.'

The last remark revived Kate's spirits like magic. She sighed. 'No,' and added retrospectively, 'we *did* have a good honeymoon, didn't we? It was exciting. I can't somehow imagine Cass and–' She broke off as Rick interposed quickly, 'Cassie and Jon rolling off a bed on top of each other–'

Kate flushed, recalling what a comical yet wildly passionate interlude that had been.

'I wasn't thinking of that,' she said stiffly, wishing that just for once her husband could concentrate on the romantic rather than the amusing episodes of their first night together.

'I know you weren't. I know what you were thinking. A touch of envy. Yes?'

'*Envy.* Good heavens what *do* you mean?'

Rick's eyebrows arched; his voice had an ironic touch as he said, 'Don't try and fool me, darling. Let's always be honest with each other, shall we? Believe me, I perfectly understand your wishing *I* was the Hon. Jon, instead of just plain Rick Ferris.'

'That's not true.'

'It won't be in time,' he asserted. 'And the sooner you speed up the forgetting business the better – for both of us.'

'I wish you wouldn't talk that way. Almost threatening. It's mean of you.'

He laughed. 'Threatening? My dear sweet girl, I never threaten. I can *act* when I have to, but only under extreme provocation.'

Not knowing whether he was serious or not, she asked, 'Such as–?'

'Putting a naughty girl over my knee if I suspected she was up to anything I didn't approve of – such as planning any secret intrigue with another woman's husband. But don't worry love, I'm sure you're not that stupid.'

She sighed. 'I don't know what's got into you. You insisted on me going to the wedding, so I went. I didn't want to – I find it all rather boring. It was just to please you, and all the thanks I get is being talked to as though I was a child. *Why?*'

The ironic smile died from his face suddenly. He took a step forward and took her face between his hands, forcing her eyes to stare up into the burning glow of his own.

'Perhaps because I love thee too much, Kate,' he said thickly.

'Oh, Rick.'

His lips travelled from her neck to the firm white curve of her shoulder above the lavender silk of her dress.

'Try to love me, Kate,' he said. 'Be faithful. That's all I ask.'

The seed of longing in her suddenly erupted to wild desire.

He carried her to the bed. And that night a child was conceived.

On the same evening at Charnbrook the newly married couple were facing complications in their relationship that neither had visualized. They were to travel to the Continent the following day and motivated by eager desire on Jon's side, went to bed early. The room was tastefully decorated in pink and cream, with antique walnut furnishings, rose brocade curtains and hangings, thickly piled carpet, and roses arranged in a crystal bowl on a Louis Quatorze side-table. The air was thick with a perfume that momentarily was too heady for Cassandra's already overwrought nerves. Just inside the door she stiffened for some moments, until Jon gently took her arm and urged her in.

'Come along, darling,' he said. 'What's the matter? Frightened?' He laughed softly. 'There's no need to be any more. We're together now, just you and me. No more prying eyes or good wishes and stupid jokes. There's always a lot of bla-bla and back slapping at weddings. But you were wonderful. And you looked simply – gorgeous.'

He caught his breath, feeling the urge swelling strong in his loins and whole body, hardly able to resist pulling the constricting chiffon dress and endless petticoats from her body – wanting – with the natural lust of any healthy young bridegroom for a young wife – to make her truly his with their flesh merging into the wild sweetness of pulsing consummation.

She said nothing, simply stood staring wide-eyed at the luxurious interior, one slender hand pressed over a breast.

'Cassie–' Jon said in a low voice, 'come on now–' and when she still didn't move, continued with a hint of impatience, 'what's the matter? Are you cold or something? Well, we'll soon remedy that.' A look of confusion crossed his face. He pulled her to the soft luxurious bed and sat upon it, bouncing up and down once or twice. 'It's soft and warm, feel it.' He jerked her wrist. She resisted, then fell beside him.

'Don't Jon – please don't.'

'Don't what? For Heaven's sake. Are you – are you tiddly? Was the champagne too much for you? It shouldn't have been. You hardly had any. Well? *Well?* Cassie – Cassie.' He pulled her close, one hand reaching for the fastening at her waist, the other firm against the subtle curves of buttocks and thighs beneath the voluminous layers of soft material.

There was a shrill cry of, 'No – *no*. Don't–' as she resisted, struggling against him, and with a violent movement freed herself. Jon stared at her, shocked and outraged by the rigid young figure confronting him. Her cheeks were flaming, her eyes wide, blazing with something he couldn't understand – a kind of cold terror like that of some wild creature in confrontation.

'What the devil–' He broke off as her breathing quickened and the colour gradually drained from her face leaving it pale and tremulous. Her under lip quivered; she lifted both hands, covering her eyes. There was the sound of a muffled sob and the glimmer of tears between the slim fingers.

'I'm sorry, Jon – oh – I'm sorry. It's just–'

Through outrage and frustration, a seed of pity stirred and pierced his desire. She looked so defenceless suddenly, like a confused child in her mass of finery with hair half tumbled to her shoulders. Sexual need withered and died in him like a flame gone cold and dead in a freezing wind.

'It's all right,' he said, 'you're tired and tense. I understand.'

'Do you? *Do* you?' But he doesn't, she thought, how could he? She didn't even understand herself, except for the shadowy terror from the past – the 'thing' that had always haunted her from her earliest youth – something only half formulated in the deepest recesses of memory, but that was always there, waiting to assume shape once the barriers in her brain collapsed. And then – she shivered. Why should it be *now,* of all times, when she so needed love and compassion from Jon of all people – the one person who'd rescued her from a dull existence to give happiness and meaning to her life?

He reached for her hand, and said quietly, 'I'm your husband, Cassie – there's no need to be afraid. We'll sort all things out later, when we've got to know each other – properly, I mean. If you like, I'll sleep in the dressing-room tonight. Tomorrow it will be different. We'll be away from here, in a new place meeting fresh people. Then, all in good time, I'll be able to show you what it's all about – marriage and loving. Smile now, dry your eyes.'

She relaxed; her lips softened and tilted sweetly, tremulously, resurrecting the fragile beauty that had so enchanted him from the moment of their first meeting. He felt again a stiffening of sensual desire, and dropped her hand, saying gruffly, 'I'll leave you to it. The night's your own. I can bed down on my own, but I'll be back in the early hours so there's no gossip.'

He turned away from her, walked stiffly to the bed and took up his silk pyjamas laid out so carefully by her own gossamer nightdress.

Very softly behind him, he heard her saying, 'I *do* love you, Jon.'

'Yes. Well – that's all right. Don't try to explain now. I guess we're both tired. And words don't help.'

She watched him with a sense of failure as he crossed the floor to the door of the small adjoining room, opened it, and went through, with his night clothes over his arm.

There was the sound of a key being turned, and she was alone.

The scent of flowers seemed everywhere – heavy, smothering and seductively sweet. Yet she knew that if he returned that evening everything would be the same. If he attempted to invade her privacy or touch her in a certain way she would scream.

Perhaps, as he'd said, tomorrow would be different. Oh, she did hope and pray so, because it was true what she'd said – she did love him; he was her heroic symbol of a legendary knight in shining armour and would always remain so.

That, perhaps, was the root of the trouble.

Her knowledge of what real life could bring had been tarnished from the very beginning.

3

During the honeymoon Jon succeeded gently and tactfully in bringing his wife to a certain acceptance of her marital obligations. It wasn't an easy process, but once her first initial objections were overcome she managed to assume a façade of pleasure in the dark, which did not fool him for a moment. Inwardly, he still felt thwarted with a sense of betrayal that was only diverted during the daytime by sight-seeing and touring the numerous cities and points of interest through Europe. Outwardly he managed a veneer of politeness and courtesy that completely deluded her. She enjoyed strolling by his side, white-gloved hand on his arm, through ornamental gardens, visiting galleries, and attending colourful operas and ballet, wearing the elegant outfits of her new wardrobe. She became well aware of her dainty charm, the admiring glances of other men and envy of women as they passed. This experience was exhilarating. When the time came to retire for nights at the expensive hotels where they stayed, she steeled herself for the enforced charade ahead, the interlude of acting a passion she did not feel. Had Jon been willing to caress her only, proximity would have been a comfort – because she *did* love him, she did, she did, she told herself frequently. But the rest – the physical intimacy was ugly, an acute pain to her.

At intervals Jon succeeded in persuading himself that time must surely heal sexual chill. He had married her expecting a mutual flowering from their love. But in the bedroom as the days passed there was nothing natural about her until she fell asleep. Neither did it seem possible completely to penetrate her virginity

The knowledge, whenever he faced it, not only humiliated but angered him. Some day, he determined, there'd have to be a down-to-earth confrontation or solution.

But as spring turned towards young summer dappling the forest with the pale green and gold of growing things, misted with bluebells, everything between Cassandra and Jon was the same – outwardly.

They lived then at the Dower House on the Charnbrook estate. It had been modernized and newly decorated and furnished for their return from the Continent. Through Walter's generous wedding present no expense had been spared. Emily had been a little ironic when he'd made his intentions clear to her. 'You're treating her as though she was your own daughter,' she once said critically. 'Almost as well as Kate. Is that quite right, do you think? It isn't as though we know Jon Wentworth that much – hardly at all. Only the money bags may be tempting him; you never know.'

Walter wagged a finger at her. 'It's not like you to be uncharitable, love. Tell you the truth I've always felt sorry for that girl. Can't have had much fun in life – pushed about from one place to another, then ending up with that stiff-necked cousin of mine and her 'do-good' husband.'

'She had a respectable upbringing,' Emily

said primly, 'and breaks with us at Beechlands.'

'Just a few weeks a year,' Walter reminded his wife, 'and between you and me I don't reckon our Kate's been much help to her.'

'So now you're criticizing our own daughter.'

Walter chuckled. 'No, my dear. Just putting things into proportion, or trying to. You can't deny that Kate's likely to overshadow any other girl in her company.'

'Well – she failed with Jon Wentworth, nevertheless,' Emily retorted sharply. 'I was pretty sure those two would end up together. Kate and Jon. A mother can sense these things, and at one time we *do* know Kate was infatuated.'

'Until Ferris came along and snapped her up from under his nose.'

'So it appears,' Emily agreed. 'But I shall never be quite easy in my mind about what happened there. It was something at the dance–'

'Oh, you women,' Walter retorted, 'always ready to make a mystery of things. There's no mystery there; the two got together –

Ferris and Kate – and that was that. A good match if you ask me. He's the means and strong character to keep her contented and in good order. And that's what our girl needs. As for Cassie' – he shrugged – 'she'll not let the Wentworths down. She's a malleable shy little thing. They'll soon have her shaped to what they want. So stop fussing and worrying, woman.'

'*Emily*,' came the reply sharply. 'I'm not just your *woman*.'

Walter grinned. 'You are, always have been and always will be,' he said affectionately, giving her a warm kiss on the cheek.

Emily smiled.

Any slight difference of opinion or argument they had usually ended that way. It had been the same from the beginning of their marriage when he was twenty and she only seventeen. But then, though humbly born, he was a natural charmer without having to resort to subtlety. You knew where you were with him. His goals in life might have been difficult but he'd gone straight for them, blunt and straightforward, with a genial twinkle in his eye, always ready to take the sting out of his victory when he won a point over a rival, socially or in business.

'Rough soil may have bred him,' a highly born member of Lynchester county council had once said when Walter won a seat on it, 'but he's a clever one – Walter Barrington. Better as a friend than an enemy.'

Which was true.

Emily recognized that his remarks concerning the suitability of Kate's marriage to Rick were probably correct. Their daughter *did* need a strong man to guide and maybe control her if the occasion arose, but being a woman she also delved a little deeper, and sensed the hidden romantic streak still lurking somewhere unappeased beneath Kate's bright façade. Still, if and when they had a child, maybe any previous yearnings for a fairytale, more sentimental, union would be erased. She'd be too occupied – hopefully – with the full-time business of motherhood.

Kate herself was unsure of her feelings on the subject. She was not basically the passionately motherly type, and when she'd heard the doctor's verdict – following an interview dealing with a number of minor ailments – that she was pregnant, her first reaction had been of mild shock. It was the natural outcome of lovemaking, of course, and she and Rick were both vital healthy individuals. But so *soon!* She'd looked forward to an immediate future of social events, travelling perhaps, and if Rick could tear himself away from his endless business and newspaper commitments – perhaps a season in London, theatre-going, and the opportunity of displaying her charm and beauty to the Press and important tycoons and people he mixed with.

Instead she'd have to face a gradual thickening of her slim figure and restriction of certain physical activities she'd hitherto enjoyed. There'd be *diet* to consider, and people fussing about her health enforcing a limited existence that would have no fun in it any more. Once the baby was born of course she'd love it and take pride in showing it off to friends and acquaintances, provided it had charm and no defects. But giving birth was a chancy business. You never *knew*, did you? With her usual buoyancy she generally managed quickly to dismiss such a morbid trend of thought; and of course Rick was delighted by the news. 'A son!' he exclaimed jubilantly. 'A boy to carry on the Ferris name. My darling, we must celebrate.'

'And suppose it's a girl?' Kate queried a trifle tartly, irritated by Rick's conventional reaction.

'If it's a girl she'll be a joy, just the same. We could call her Gwenna or Marged. Welsh.'

Kate pouted. 'I'm not sure I like those. And anyway – it's a long time ahead yet. Six months. A lot can happen before then.'

A shadow crossed Rick's face. 'What do you mean by that?'

'Nothing. *Nothing*. Only you *do* take things so much for granted. It's I who've got to go through it all. Men are so – so fatuous somehow, so self-centred–'

'And how much do you know of men, my darling? In the plural?' His voice was teasing. She managed to smile.

'That's better. That's my Kate.' He kissed

her, and she relaxed. But inwardly there was a tiny seed of resentment.

Shortly following this conversation Rick informed her he was going up to London for a week to meet an American tycoon who was on a visit to London for discussions including the future of the moving picture business currently sweeping the States and the possibilities of co-operation with Ferris in the publication of a weekly paper, *Pictorial Review,* to be bought on both sides of the Atlantic.

It sounded exciting.

'Take me with you,' said Kate quickly. 'Oh, *please* Rick, I should so enjoy it–'

She broke off as he shook his head, 'I'm afraid not this time. I shall be putting up at my club. It will be a strictly business affair. No pleasure jaunts or gadding around.'

'We needn't *gad* at all,' Kate said stubbornly. 'And I wouldn't interfere with your – business whatever it is. I should be perfectly happy to wander about London a bit on my own. We could stay at some quiet hotel, and in the mornings–'

Rick interrupted with a negative gesture of

his hand and a sharp 'No.'

'But–'

His jaws tightened determinedly. 'I mean what I say. Some other time. I promise you, we'll go up to town together and have a few days, although it's not so long since we were there, is it?' He smiled reminiscently.

'The honeymoon? That was different. It's mean of you, Rick. Especially now – when I've – when–'

'Yes?'

'When I've just told you about the baby. You were pleased about that; it isn't much to ask in return.'

'Kate, there's no point in arguing. I'd have no time with you at all, and I wouldn't dream of leaving you to get into mischief by yourself while I was cooped up discussing facts and figures and plans with this American who could play an extremely important part in our future. So *please* be reasonable and take that glum look off your face. It doesn't suit you; another thing, I should have thought you'd have wanted a bit of peace yourself at such a time. It's April now – the weather's good – just right to laze

116

about a bit and from what I've heard most women who are expecting' – he gave a grin – 'pardon me – enceinte – like the chance of being alone to dream and pamper themselves.'

Kate flounced and turned away. 'Oh, bother being "enceinte" – such a *stupid* expression anyway. And I think it's perfectly horrid of you. Unfair.'

'Perhaps,' he agreed blandly. 'If you want to see it that way, do so. It won't make a scrap of difference. As far as I'm concerned the matter's finished, I'm going to town on male business for a week and you're staying here.'

'You say male business. Does that include Mrs Linda Wade?'

'If her advice is needed. But I rather think not. In any case, dear heart, you won't have to endure her company.'

Kate bit her lip and succeeded in stifling a sudden show of irrational jealousy.

And there presumably the matter ended.

Rick went to London, and Kate stayed at Woodgate.

Feeling bored, slightly disorientated and

frustrated, she took a wander one day in a vague direction towards Cassandra's retreat and round a bend of a lane saw a scarlet two-seater car parked by a gate leading into a field. She paused, wondering if it was Jon's and whether or not to turn back. Before she'd decided, he cut from the woods, and walked towards her. He was casually dressed, and hatless. The pale sunlight lit his fair hair, and emphasized the easy swing of his athletic body through the lacy thin shadows of the trees. In spite of her determination to show nothing but cold politeness, Kate's heart gave a lurch. He looked so handsome and so young.

'Hullo,' he said, hand outstretched. 'Good to see you Kate.'

She offered the tips of her fingers answering, and his own were strong round her palm. She noticed then, at close quarters, he did not appear *quite* so young as she'd at first thought. His mouth was somehow slightly strained and his blue eyes looked tired.

She'd meant merely to say 'Good morning, Jon,' affecting indifferent recognition, but instead just answered, 'Yes. Hullo.'

'Haven't seen you for ages. Only once since the – the wedding – that day in Woodgate. You were with Rick. Remember?'

She nodded. 'Rick asked you in for a drink, but you refused.'

'I had to get back. I'd promised Cass.'

'How is Cassandra?' The question came out with difficulty.

'Oh, fine – *fine* – as far as I know. I mean she's not complained of anything wrong – except for her painting, of course.' His voice held a bitter note.

'*That*? But she loves it.'

'I know. That's the point; she never has enough time for it. First thing every morning and she's off to that place. I've dropped her there now. She's in the middle of some imaginative thing that I just can't fathom. But maybe you'll be able to make it out. I take it that's where you're going now?'

'I'd no plan exactly. But I will now you've mentioned it.'

'Good.' His face lit up perceptively. 'I shall see you again then? I'm calling for her in about an hour. Yes?'

'That depends,' Kate replied.

'On what? Your – husband?'

Kate shook her head. 'No, no. Rick's in London, on business.'

'How neglectful of him – and rather stupid,' Jon said pointedly.

Kate flushed. 'Not at all. The business includes something very important, and–'

'Mrs Wade?'

Kate's temper rose. 'What a thing to say. Of course not. And you've no right to suggest – suggest that those old stories were true. As a matter of fact, I've already met her socially at Woodgate, our home. She's extremely knowledgeable and her experience is invaluable to Rick over some matters.'

'I'm sure it is,' Jon agreed meaningfully.

Kate glared at him, then said, 'I don't like your attitude, and if I'm going to see Cass I must go. It's quite a way.'

Jon lifted an arm. 'Oh, I'm sorry. I didn't want to upset you. But – you look so lovely when you're in a temper, Kate. You know that, don't you?'

'I know you shouldn't be speaking like

that, and that it's a stupid interview,' Kate retorted. 'Please let me pass.'

He shrugged and stepped aside. She swept by, but could sense his gaze still on her as she took the turn into the wood.

Cassandra was standing at the opening to the studio when Kate arrived there. She was looking picturesque in a long black skirt embroidered at the hem, with a fringed paisley shawl draped round her shoulders. Her hair was loose, spilling like a pale gold fan over her arms. She had a look of contemplation on her face as though thinking out an idea for a fresh painting. Behind her the luminous green depths of one of the woodland pools – said to have been worked in ancient times as slate pits – glittered translucently through the morning light. Silver birches quivered amid the darker tracery of thorn, elder, and oak, which were shadowed by the spreading branches of a large beech on the other side. The whole scene had the atmosphere momentarily of some legend or fairytale.

Then Cassandra spoke. 'Oh, hullo Kate.' She lifted a hand to one breast as though startled. 'I didn't expect you.'

'Am I intruding? I came this way by chance, and met Jon. He told me you were here so I thought I'd look in. He said you were doing a lot of painting now.'

'Oh, you *saw* him!'

'Yes. He looked a bit tired, I thought.'

Cassandra shrugged. 'He's very busy with the estate – always on the go. The Wentworths' bailiff has retired now, he's too old and they've given him the lodge to live in with his wife. So Jon's taken over – temporarily, he says. But I don't know. I think there's a question of money involved. And of course since he left Oxford Jon's had no particular post – he did history, you know, at university – but he doesn't seem to want to teach. So–' She shrugged lightly. 'Well would *you*? If you were him, with all this?'

'I have no idea what I'd want to do if I was Jon,' Kate replied shortly. 'But about your paintings – aren't you going to show me, now I've trailed all the way here?'

'Of course.' Cassandra turned and went ahead to the newly installed door, pushing through undergrowth and brambles, leaving

Kate to follow.

Inside a number of sketches, drawings and watercolours were heaped against one wall. Cassandra's cape lay over a chair, and an assortment of painting materials were on a table. There was an evocative odd smell of wood, mixed with that of turpentine, and a painting was propped on an easel near the far end of the room – a portrait of a girl with luminous large eyes staring from a pale heart-shaped face. She appeared to be wearing a nun's habit. No hair was visible, but in a brilliant stream of light from the window the effect of the pale skin, and finely drawn features against the background of dark drapes and shadowed faintly defined trees was arresting, and showed a skill Kate had not thought Cassie possessed.

'Did you do that?'

'Yes. But it's not quite finished yet.'

'Who is it?'

'Just someone I met in the wood,' Cassandra answered. 'Near the pool.'

'She looks like a nun.'

'Yes. I think she comes from a priory round here.'

'Priory? A nunnery? But there isn't one. There was once, of course. The forest had quite a few religious houses in the past. But I'm sure there's only the Monastery now. I should have heard; I know. I've lived here most of my life–' She broke off, almost startled by the slight half-smile of condescension on the other girl's face. It was as though she meant to imply – you may know the lanes and footpaths, but I *belong*.

However, all Cassandra said was, 'She looked like that anyway. And I painted her; that's all.'

'Oh, well,' Kate remarked, trying to stifle the quite unreasoning sense of jealousy that rose up in her, the jealousy of 'place'. 'Perhaps she was on a visit or something. The people at Oakthorpe Farm are Catholics, and take guests sometimes. Anyway there's no priory, except ruined ones, now.'

She didn't wait to see Jon again, but left shortly after that conversation, wondering irritably if it was being pregnant that made her so resentful of Cassandra's apparent involvement with Burnwood country.

During Rick's week in London Kate did her best to involve herself with the future of motherhood. She made two trips to Lynchester, shopping occasions for the inspection of clothes designed – as glamorously as possible – for the 'young matron'. She didn't care to consider herself in feminine terms as anyone looking in the least matronly; the picture brought to her mind was mildly disagreeable, but the modistes she consulted, the beaming couturiers and dressers were so flattering, so openly envious and admiring of her beauty and how entrancing she could appear as 'the young mother', given the right styles to enhance her charm, that eventually she became relaxed and found herself enjoying being the focal point of such interest.

Rick, of course, was well known as one of the richest men in the county, probably the whole of Britain, which helped shopkeepers almost to fall over their heels to acquire her patronage. The fact also that he was so astonishingly handsome in an exciting male way, and after years of bachelorhood had eventually been lured to the altar by Walter Barrington's young daughter, had created curiosity with an undercurrent of envy that occasionally after a flattering session ended with such secret comments among sales-women as 'Yes, she's certainly good looking. But a trifle naive, don't you think? And with his experience! You can't help wondering what he saw in her.'

The wonderment was false, of course. Beneath her vitality and luscious beauty lurked something else – outrageous though indefinable, holding a sexual challenging quality that only a man of Rick's fibre could hope to control. Women could sense her peculiar magnetism as well as men, and though outwardly polite, resented it. Kate felt the undercurrent of reaction and was mildly surprised but couldn't be bothered to understand it. She was the 'young madam', wife of Rick Ferris of Woodgate House and enjoyed what she could of her new status.

So when Rick returned from London her previous reluctant mood had been mostly dispelled by a week's preening herself like some exotic bird in glorification of her fine feathers and furbelows.

Rick attempted to explain his business progress concerning the *Pictorial Review* for which he'd succeeded in acquiring the helpful backing from his American counterpart. Although dealing with news headlines from both sides of the Atlantic he told her – as he'd mentioned before – society and stage gossip would be a priority of the publication, highlighted by the quickly growing industry of moving-pictures on the screen.

Kate managed to present a show of interest which Rick soon detected was half-hearted. He was mildly amused knowing she was burning to discuss something of her own.

'Well,' he said breaking off, 'that's about it.'

'It sounds interesting, Rick.'

'And you haven't even enquired about Linda. Did I see her? Just for a quick lunch at the Ritz, that's all. Come along now, what have you been up to?'

She stared at him, faintly disappointed.

He hadn't even commented on the new gown she was wearing. It was of jade shaded silk, with drapes cunningly contrived to hide even a faint thickening of the waist. Her russet hair was drawn to the back of her head, held by invisible pins, and a tiny flowered comb that left only a few rebellious curls to fall softly against her cheeks.

She well knew she looked enchanting, why hadn't Rick noticed?

'I've been spending your – *our* money,' she said pointedly. 'On clothes. Well, what else was there to do? You don't want me to ride any more, you wouldn't take me to town with you, you didn't want me wandering about the forest alone – although I did once go and see Cass. But what else was there for me to do?'

Rick smiled; it was a curiously disarming smile, she thought, on so rugged though handsome a face.

'My dear love,' he said, 'I do apologize.'

'For what?'

'Not mentioning how very beautiful you looked. It was worth going away just to come back and find such a smart conscientious young wife waiting for me. And I do like the dress. Very becoming. You hardly need this.' He took a small box from his pocket and handed it to her. 'Still, the colour will match.'

She stared at the gift and after unwrapping it lifted the lid. Inside lay a gold brooch studded with emeralds and diamonds in the shape of a bird.

For a moment Kate was speechless. Then following a little gulp of surprise, she said, 'Oh, darling, it's lovely – *lovely*.'

She held it against her breast with the wild rich colour flooding her face. He took it gently from her hand and placed it on the table.

'I love you Kate,' he said, pulling her to him.

She almost replied, 'And I love you', but did not; she was too bewildered, almost bemused wishing for the first time that no such person as Jon Wentworth existed and that she had never met him.

Rick gave a little sigh – not merely because of her omission but because he had other things on his mind. His visit to London had

not merely been for the American amal-
gamation, but of a political nature. For
months, even years, in the background of
his mind had festered an ambition not just
for his own business advancement or
acquiring an immense fortune, but in some
way for being a voice in the foundation of a
new party at Westminster – one concerned
with those less fortunate than himself.
Being a man of the world and also
intrinsically at heart an adventurer with a
shrewd insight into human nature, he was
aware of the injustices concealed by a
veneer of 'caring' at Westminster. Liberalism
and Conservatism both had axes to grind.
Maybe all the men with an aptitude and
ambition for governing others had. He was
sufficiently honest with himself to accept
the truth that after his father's death in
Rick's twenty-first year, his ambition had
been to double the rich fortune left to his
only son. His drive and energy, shrewd
business calculations had more than
fulfilled the aim. But success once achieved
had also left a gap. It was at this point that
he'd turned his interests to other matters

and the injustices of social life. Through personal investigations and tours of poor life in cities, including Tiger Bay in Cardiff, and London's impoverished East End, he'd been shocked that human life could exist and breed in such degradation. He was not by nature a philanthropist. He enjoyed his own wealth and was no fanatic willing to squander any on hopeless causes. But a voice in the House? – ah! that was a different matter. He possessed a certain power at oratory that could well serve his inherent Welsh dramatic ability and prove useful in furthering fairer justice for the poor and the deprived.

So at the point of his meeting Kate major developing aims in his mind had been the new newspaper plans and the wild possibility of getting to Westminster and eventually with luck and his usual fire, sowing the seeds there of a new party.

Kate had momentarily allayed such zest to a minimum. Though his experience of women was considerable, he had never before been so completely swept off his feet, or wanted any of the feminine beauties languishing after him to be a wife.

But that first moment at the dance he had known.

She was the one.

More than that.

She was the only one he'd want as future mother of his children. So it had to be marriage, and he'd determined in some way he'd manage in time to wipe her wild schoolgirlish heart free of any faint sentimental yearnings for that golden boy the Hon. Jon.

So far he realized he'd half succeeded but there was a lingering faint shadow still there.

Hence the brooch that had cost him many thousands, and he knew when he saw the light in her eyes, the sudden joy of gratitude and passionate welcome, that he was on the right track.

A challenge lay ahead of him, combining his own male existence with a satisfactory love life ending any doubts at all that his wife was his completely.

No regrets or shadows from the past.

No Jon.

4

The heady sweet-scented days of spring were followed by a warm summer during which Rick made considerable effort to keep Kate contented and as satisfied as possible in her limited existence due to approaching motherhood. It was not an easy period for either of them. With Rick's enthusiasm for his new business projects still occupying much of his mind, the effort of dealing with his wife's ever-changing moods frequently chafed and caused an inner irritation which drove him to spending more than usual time at the stud or actively busying himself on the farm. After periods of physical activity in the open air he managed to put things into proportion and returned home ready to tackle Kate's complaints and unpredictable bursts of quick temper with apparent equanimity.

He thought frequently that if she had to

cope with more household matters she would feel better and life would be more harmonious. But the housekeeper, Mrs Rook, whom he'd employed for years with a competent staff, made any efforts on Kate's part in the running of the home quite super-fluous. In any case, Kate was not naturally interested in everyday chores. Except for arranging flowers and other such 'lady-like' occupations, she was completely satisfied by her nominal status as Mistress of Woodgate and content to leave domestic matters for those employed to see things ran smoothly.

Cassandra, on the other hand, had done her best at the beginning of her marriage to please Jon, and prove herself efficient in household management. But, with her humble background and no knowledge whatever of Wentworth standards and manner of living, Jon very quickly realized her shortcomings and insisted on employing a well-trained housekeeper with two other servants and a man, although at that period, finances were strained, and he could ill-afford the upkeep.

His one hope was that Cassandra in time

would be able to adjust better to her new role as wife – not only domestically, but in bed.

For months he managed outwardly to stifle his disappointments – the tormenting irritations and frustrations of which Cassandra appeared completely unaware. Romantically and sentimentally she could reciprocate. But, good God, he thought frequently, surely she couldn't be so completely ignorant of what a normal man needed and expected from a wife?

Grudgingly, he had to admit to himself that she was very like her paintings – naive and dream-like, with a childish yet effective capacity for evading down-to-earth issues. It was as though something in her was forever ready to slip away, and escape before he had a chance to confront her with any material problem.

In a sense this was true, though Jon had not the slightest idea of the reason. But Cassie knew; from the earliest days of her far-away childhood she had known, but had managed somehow to erase it from complete recognition – the terror that loomed in the past as a shadow, formless but indestructible – the 'thing' she could share with no one – not even Jon – *especially* Jon.

So the days passed, frequently tense with expectancy for Kate, dream-like for Cassandra whose visits to the Tree Studio became more frequent causing an inner irritation to Jon who only managed with difficulty to curb outbursts of quick temper.

Very occasionally he met Kate by chance, who by late August was wearing long capes to disguise her full figure, but Jon was not deceived.

'Are you aiming to become a nun, Mrs Ferris?' he asked pointedly once with a slight one-sided smile.

Kate's brows met crossly above her eyes. 'Are you intending to be insolent, Mr Wentworth?'

He gave a burst of laughter, then sobered quickly. 'Of course not. It's just that I'm getting used to the breed nowadays.'

'What breed? What do you mean?'

She hadn't intended to argue, even discuss anything with him. It was amazing to discover he still had the power to touch her emotionally in any way.

'Nuns,' he stated flatly, suddenly cold and hard-looking. 'It's Cassie, you know. She has quite a yen for them. Have you seen her little hidey-hole recently?'

'Not for some time. I don't go far these days.'

'Hm! Well, you'd be surprised, I can tell you. No longer flowers and trees and fairies – just that one woman in her cloak and cowl – do they call it? – staring by the pool – that old slate pool. In every possible pose you could think of – staring at the sky, or sitting on a rock dabbling her hand by the stream – sometimes with her arms out but always with a simpering kind of holier-than-thou expression on her face. It's not natural, that's what I say. I tell you, Kate, she's *imagining* things. There aren't any nuns around here, not now. It's just an obsession she's got, from reading so many legends, and thinking *she's* some kind of Lorelei or something – Cassie herself.' He stopped talking and looked suddenly downcast, grim.

Kate was nonplussed. 'Oh dear. I'm sorry,'

she said lamely, and this, in one way, was true. It seemed incomprehensible almost that Jon of all people, who had seemed to have everything except wealth – family, looks, and sufficient glamour to stir any feminine heart, could become so downcast by a shy, quiet little thing like Cass.

'I suppose we all have moods,' she said lamely, adding probingly, 'you – you *do* have the same interests, don't you? You and Cass? I always thought painting was one of the things that brought you together. The art – and – and that sort of thing?'

'Did you indeed!' The sarcasm in his voice almost shocked her. 'It rather depends on what *kind* of art, I'd say.'

'Oh well, it's none of my business,' Kate said rather shortly. 'I must be getting back.' She brushed past him and heard him saying as she moved through the trees, 'You always seem to be "getting back" – I'm surprised Ferris doesn't put a halter about your shoulders.'

With her cheeks flaming she wheeled round quickly and said, 'But you're not Rick. Anyway if you did, I'd slap your face.'

Her heart was hammering as she half stumbled over some briars. He caught up with her in one bound and placed a hand on her arm. She stood still, rigid with a conflict of emotion. 'Oh Kate – Kate – you know I didn't mean it,' he said softly against her ear. 'Be nice to me, Kate, I'm not a happy man at the moment.'

The temper died in her and, sensing it, he tweaked a curl nestling over her temple. She pushed his hand away. 'You mustn't, Jon–'

'Why not? We're cousins, aren't we?'

She shook her head. 'You know we're not, nor ever could be. And if we were – even then – nothing could make this sort of thing right, I'm Rick's wife.'

'And I'm–'

'Cassie's husband.'

'And if I wasn't?'

'It would be just the same.'

But would it?

This was the question that nagged her as she made her way back to Woodgate. Why was it so difficult sometimes to know what was right and what was wrong? Perhaps if she'd not been with child – but was it just *because* of her pregnancy that she still so easily got emotionally confused? It would have been so simple during that short interlude with Jon to have put her arms round him in an effort to comfort and ease away the bitterness – so wonderful to run her hands through his crisp blond hair – to let their tears mingle, and then ease his loneliness away. This was a sensation she'd never felt before. Was it just the motherliness in her? Or something stronger in her that just wouldn't die?

I hope Rick's back, she thought, as she quickened her footsteps. I mustn't doubt like this. I'm having his baby; I'm his wife.

But even when she lay with him that night, for a long time she remained restless and awake.

One of Kate's grumbles during the late summer and autumn months of pregnancy was boredom. As the time for the baby's birth drew nearer Rick became more stubborn in curtailing her activities.

'If only we could go to London for a weekend – you *did* promise,' she said.

'Later,' he always said, 'when everything's over.'

'You mean the baby. That means months ahead. It would be different if we could have moved – gone somewhere else to live, somewhere with proper grounds. It isn't as if you couldn't afford it. There's nowhere to walk here except that square of lawn at the back and the rose garden. It's such an ordinary *dated* sort of house. So *Victorian.*'

'So are we. It was my father's choice; he had it built to his own design. It's considered an extremely fine combination of Jacobean and nineteenth-century style.'

'But we are so near the road. Why couldn't there have been a pool or something, and little copses and terraces?'

'So that you could tumble down them? Anyway, I didn't realize before you had such a keen sense of architecture or liking for ornate grounds.'

'Not ornate. That's what I think is so – well, tasteless somehow, about Woodgate – the pointed roofs and long square chimneys, a strange mixture–' She broke off with a sigh. 'I wish–'

'I know what you're wishing,' he interrupted curtly. 'For an ancient stately home similar to the Wentworths' – somewhere traditionally grand-looking surrounded by hundreds of useless acres, inconveniently situated as far from Lynchester as possible. Well, my darling, you'd better forget it. This place suits me. Easily accessible to the city for quick business meetings and on the very edge of the forest. There's the farm, and the stud. Good God! Why can't you be satisfied?'

She pouted. 'You just don't understand.'

'I understand perfectly. You have a mania for being spoiled. Well – I'm willing to oblige, up to a point. You've got the whole of the second floor already redecorated and furnished to your taste for the baby and the nursery quarters. You have a nanny and staff booked to take charge when the time arrives. If there's anything else you can think up, you've only to say. And' – he smiled with a hint of mischief – 'I'll give it my most serious consideration. Just so long as you – behave, like a good girl and young wife should.'

'Oh!' Suddenly irritated, she flounced away. 'Don't talk to me as though I was a child. Sometimes I hate you–'

He strode after her and caught her to him. 'No you don't, Mrs Ferris. And one day I'll make you take that back. One day I'll make you love me.'

For a moment his lips were firm and hot on hers, then he released her quickly and strode from the room.

For some inexplicable reason she wanted to cry, although she could not say why.

Early in November of that year, Kate surprisingly gave birth to twin girls. Rick, who'd expected and looked forward to having a son, was nevertheless delighted. Kate's first reaction was of shock.

'*Two?*' she gasped when the tiny babies were shown to her. '*Mine? Both* of them?'

When the truth had sunk in, and she'd recovered sufficient strength to study them she could still feel nothing but astonishment. She had no rush of motherly love or desire to suckle them or have them close. All she wanted was to be quiet and sleep, away from the quaint monkey-faced little creatures who made her feel as though she was in the midst of a squawking menagerie.

She was extremely exhausted. The double birth had not been easy and she half-hoped she'd slip into unconsciousness then wake up and find none of the last hours had happened, and that she was back in her bedroom at Beechlands, her old home.

For the next two days she was lethargic and appeared to take little interest in the babies, feeding them only when necessary, then wanting them taken back to their frilly cots. Rick did all he could to cheer her with lavish gifts and compliments, praising her courage, and the beauty of his daughters. She took no notice.

Then, suddenly, on the third day she came alive again, and for the first time since their arrival, smiled.

The nurse had just left the room, and Rick was standing at the bedside. Kate finally touched the forehead of one baby peeping from its white shawl. 'Aren't they funny little things?' she said.

'They're beautiful,' he answered, 'and so are you.'

'Now don't flatter. I must look a sight. I'm sorry I've been such a dreary thing – and I'm sorry one isn't a boy. I know you wanted a son–'

'My dear love, I wouldn't change these two for any male Ferris in the world.' There was a pause before he said, 'Plenty of time ahead for–' He broke off.

Her expression clouded. 'For what? Go on, tell me, but don't expect me to go through all this again.'

'Of course not,' he said. 'I don't expect anything from you you don't want yourself. At the moment all you've got to do is to take things easily and get your strength back. That's the priority always – to be my own lovely tantalizing wife again.'

But she knew he was merely evading the issue, and because of her drained energy half-dreaded the future.

The babies were in no way identical. One was dark-eyed with a tuft of reddish dark hair, the other light brown and more fragile-looking.

'My mother was fairish when she was young,' Kate said one day when she and

Rick were pondering over them. 'The other one – well, she'll probably have very dark hair when she's older, like you.'

'A Ferris?' One of his eye-brows shot up whimsically. 'Poor little blighter. What will we call them then? We never settled for names.'

'I wondered about Felicity for the fair one.'

'*Felicity?* Where did that come from?'

'I don't quite know. But I like it – it means happiness.'

'Felicity Ferris? Hm.'

'You think it's silly?'

'No. Just a bit fancy. However, what about the other one?'

'Your turn, Rick.'

His answer was immediate. 'Marged?'

'Marged?' she echoed the word softly.

'It was my mother's name. Welsh. Remember?'

'Oh. Well, yes, of course, if you want; it has a kind of darkness in it – just as Felicity seems sort of light and sunshiny – a bit ethereal. Marged has a rich colour like forest trees in the autumn, and sunset on

146

dark, still pools.' She broke off, smiling faintly. 'I suppose I sound a bit silly - sentimental. But I think now I like Marged very much. I'm a bit sleepy though, Rick, so let's leave it for the moment, and then have another think.'

The result of this conversation was that a month later the twins were christened in Lynchester Cathedral as Felicity and Marged Ferris.

In February, out of courtesy, and as a family gesture, presumably to celebrate the birth of the Ferris twins and the first anniversary of Jon's marriage to Cassandra, the Barringtons and Rick and Kate were invited to Charnbrook for dinner.

'It must be done, William,' Olivia said resignedly. 'Not only as a show of good manners, but to find out what we can about the relationship between our son and that silly girl he married. Things aren't right, you know. Jon isn't at all like he once was – so short-tempered and on edge. I've done my best to draw him out, but he was almost rude to me the other day, and as for

Cassandra herself – I wonder sometimes if there's something seriously wrong with her. Mentally, I mean – she's so vague and whenever I try to get to grips with any problem there could be, she puts that sly smile on her face and says, "We're quite happy, Lady Olivia. Jon and I love each other".' She frowned. 'But I don't believe that young woman has a shred of feeling in her.'

'Hm.' Sir William took a pull on his pipe. 'You must do as you think fit, my dear. Have the dinner party by all means, although what chance there'll be for any private conversation's doubtful, I'd say. Still, a show of good feeling will be all to the good. I owe quite a bit to Barrington at the moment. Had bad luck with another lot of shares – Pelham & Company – only the other week, and Walter very kindly put his hand in his pocket for me.'

'Oh William! Why do you take such risks? Spending what we haven't got and having to rely on people like the Barringtons to get you out of a hole!'

'Knowing us more than pays him, Olivia.

Not so many of our breed about these days.'

Olivia sighed. 'It seems nothing will change you. But on this I am *determined*. I'm going to discover what is wrong with Jonathan.'

'Do, do. Give your dinner party, put on a good show, and I'll somehow contrive to see you two mothers have a chance of a chin-wag. Women have a better nose for these things than men.'

So the event was arranged, and invitations sent to the Barringtons and Ferrises.

Kate at first wanted to refuse and searched for an excuse. But Rick, as usual, was determined to accept.

'Only a week or two ago you were complaining that nothing happened, that you were tired of seeing just "babies and bottles",' he reminded her. 'Now there's a chance of dressing up to the eyes and showing off your new slender figure again, you go stubborn and want to decline. Well, my darling, you'll do as I say for once, and I mean it – even if I have to drag you by the hair of your head.'

'You brute!'

'Exactly. To tell you the truth, Kate, I'm getting somewhat tired of your tantrums lately. Another thing – don't let me overhear you threatening to slap either of my daughters again. I heard you the other day; Marged, wasn't it? Oh, I realize she can be a wilful little thing, and I don't suppose you meant it for a moment. But if you ever raise a hand against either of the twins, and I get to know of it – it's you who'll get the slapping. So remember it.'

Kate wheeled round on him.

'You've no right to talk like that, even in fun. You–'

'Oh, I can assure it wasn't fun, my love–'

'Anyhow,' she interrupted, 'you want me interested in the twins all the time, although I'm not allowed to *do* anything for them; oh, no, We have a nanny and servants for that. Am I just supposed to look *on* them? Without a right to say a word or use a touch of discipline when it's necessary?'

'I didn't say that. At the moment they're only babies, Kate. I realize Marged's a bit of a bawler – it's just high spirits. I guess you were the same at her age – maybe a bit worse.'

'I was supposed to be a very good baby,' Kate told him primly.

He laughed. 'And some say "pigs can fly". Now–' his voice softened, 'forget this silly argument, just concentrate on counting your blessings and think about what you're going to wear for the "get-together".'

She eventually chose soft luscious velvet in a deep lilac shade with a flimsy chiffon shawl spotted with diamante for her shoulders. She had a single flower in her piled-up hair that curled in a fringe over her forehead, and round her white neck wore a diamond necklace, one of Rick's gifts to her.

They arrived at Charnbrook shortly before seven; and the Wentworth family and Barringtons were already gathered in the drawing-room when Kate was taken down by a maid from the powder room to join them.

It was then that Kate received her first shock.

Cassandra.

She was seated near to Mrs Barrington on a high-backed satin-upholstered chair at the far end of the room facing the door as Lady

Wentworth moved, hand extended, to greet Rick and his wife. The men were gathered by the massive marble fireplace, including Jon, who looked distinctly ill-at-ease. And no wonder, thought Kate, considering Cassandra's appearance. She was attired all in black – a high-necked dress, with a cape-like arrangement falling over the shoulders, and a spreading skirt covering the tips of her shoes. Her light hair was dragged to the back of her head almost entirely covered by black lace veiling resembling a miniature mantilla, of some religious order perhaps. Kate's nerves lurched. Over the dark bodice of the gown a pearl cross hung at the breast from a silver chain.

The whole effect – the demure severity of expression on the pale face against the unrelieved black was startling, and some-how macabre.

Kate went forward mechanically, forcing a smile.

'Hullo, Cass, how are you?'

'Perfectly well, thank you,' Cassandra answered in high sweet tones. 'And how are you?'

'Me? Oh, I'm all right. I haven't seen you lately.'

'No. I've been busy.'

'Painting?'

'Yes, and other things.'

'Cass doesn't make a habit of mingling with us normal folk these days,' Jon said sarcastically, coming to join them. 'She is much too pure.' Instantly he regretted the cruel comment, but it was too late.

An embarrassed flush rose to Kate's cheeks. She was wondering wildly what to say, whether to make a joke of Jon's rebuff or change the conversation quickly into other channels, when Lady Wentworth mercifully intervened.

'Do come and sit down, my dear,' she said to Kate. 'I was just saying to your dear mama that I hadn't seen your delightful babies since the christening. One day you must bring them along in the afternoon, and we can have a cosy cup of tea together without these wicked men of ours.' Her smile at Kate was as sugar sweet as her brief frown at Jon was strong with warning.

Of Cassie, whose wedding anniversary it

was, she took no notice at all.

The whole short interlude had the atmosphere of a social drama being enacted on a stage with no one knowing quite what the climax was to be, a situation saved only by a veneer of good manners, and the good food and wine that followed.

Actually such an assessment would have been correct, although it was three hours before the finale took shape, and one which neither the Wentworths nor Barringtons could have anticipated.

By 10.30 the guests had departed. Jon and Cassandra were the last to leave after a cold farewell from Lady Wentworth and a gruff 'Hope all's well with you two – have a good night m'boy', from Sir William.

Two bright spots of colour burned on Olivia's high cheek-bones as she returned to the dining-room followed by her husband. A fire was still burning brightly, the air was warm; small signs of festivity remained there – massed bowls of roses, a large framed photograph of Jon and Cassandra on their wedding day standing in a silver frame on a side table. Light leaped from logs and coal, catching the glint of wall lamps and the immense crystal chandelier hanging from the high encrusted ceiling. Soft shadows mingled with the rich warm scent of the flowers evocative of bygone romantic luxury. A gentle tune from a French china clock upheld by baby angels tinkled merrily from the mantelshelf. But Oliver Wentworth's face was grim. The very atmosphere seemed to chill as she spoke.

'Outrageous. That girl's behaviour was quite inexcusable. To appear like that – making a mockery of her marriage to our son. And in front of those – those Barringtons. So demure and sly. As if she was in *mourning*. Or about to enter a convent. We must do something William. It can't go on. Jon has aged years, even in the short time since they moved to the Dower House. We must have advice. Marriages can be annulled in certain cases. I'm sure something's very wrong. In cases like this–' She broke off, lifting a shred of lace handkerchief to one eye, her upper lip trembled beneath her long aristocratic nose.

William patted her shoulder comfortingly.

'There, there, m'dear. Compose yourself. It's not as bad as all that. Young couples often go through a tricky stage. And it's my belief he still thinks the world of her. Give them time, that's what I say, give them time.'

'Oh. You always take the easy way out,' his wife complained irritably. 'What help is that?'

'Sometimes it's the only course left. Try and get things in proportion. She didn't do anything *wrong*, did she? Not as if she behaved objectionably, or drank too much. The dress was a bit gloomy-looking, I grant you. But some women think black's smart these days–'

'She wasn't thinking of smartness. It would be a lot better if she did. Sometimes I really believe she's not quite all there. And with *Jon* for a husband. My only son.'

'Hm! Yes! I'll have a word with him tomorrow. Maybe he should take a stronger line with her in some way – wake her up a bit and give her an idea of what being a Wentworth means. I thought in the beginning she'd take to horse riding. But the first fall ended it. Well, you either like horses or you don't. The point is, Olivia, she's Jon's wife, and somehow we've got to come to terms. Don't worry, my dear. I've a shrewd idea he may be having a word with her tonight. He'd a firm set to his face when he left. He no more liked her dreary get-up than we did. Don't know why he allowed it.'

'I'm sure he didn't. If you remember Jon came first tonight. She'd been at the Barringtons for the afternoon and arrived with them. I should have thought that woman – Barrington's wife – would have used what influence she had to stop such a charade. That's what it was you know, just a charade with that silent, silly little creature apeing a Spanish duenna or some foreign nun. I really am upset. I feel quite ill in fact–'

Sir William sighed. 'Oh, come now, Olivia. Enough's enough. Damned if I'm going to waste any more breath over a black dress. Pull yourself together. Take a pill or something or a hot toddy and get to bed. I'm having a last smoke then I'll join you.'

At the time William was having his smoke,

Jon was confronting Cassandra in their bedroom at the Dower House.

She had removed the veiling from her hair and was sitting before the dressing-table mirror regarding herself solemnly through the glass. The shadowed lamplight made the reflection of her eyes enormous in her pale face, but Jon steeled himself for what he was about to say and do. 'Come here, Cass. Get up. Look at me.'

She turned her head questioningly. 'What is it? What do you want? I'm tired.'

'I said get up.'

She sighed, and got to her feet. 'Jon, I–'

He came forward and put one hand on a shoulder and with the other clutched the fastening of her bodice, took the chain from her neck and threw it across the room. She pulled back, but lips were warm against her throat, his voice was already husky, when he said, 'I'm going to love you tonight, Cass – properly, not like it's been before – but sweet and deep. *Deep,* darling, as a man should love a wife. We'll have a baby, Cass–'

'No, *no.*' Her resistance held the frail high cry of some delicate captured bird. 'Jon, *please–'* but it only inflamed his desire and determination.

'It's all right, darling. Trust me.' As she struggled his mouth crushed hers; she fell back in his arms, and forcefully but gentle still, he removed the black gown, lifted and carried her to the large canopied bed and laid her down. She lay like some defenceless doll, with her pale hair spilling over the pillow as though all life had been drained from her. Rigidly she watched him disappear into the dressing-room and return only moments later in the paisley dressing-gown he'd worn on their honey-moon. His face was flushed. There was an eager look on it that made her cringe. Instinctively she crossed her arms over the white bodice of her underskirt.

He moved forward, tentatively at first, brilliant-eyed, and stood looking down on her for a moment.

'This is our marriage night, Cass,' he said. Then he opened the gown, and she saw him for a second, naked, upright and strong as a young tree reaching to the sunlight.

Something quivered to life in her,

struggled, then darkened into a spreading cloud of terror as his maleness registered. There was nothing there any more but fear – the sick engulfing thing from the past blotting out all else except a wild panic that froze the blood in her veins, leaving her rigid and powerless against a lusting tide of need that had been frustrated for too long. He became in her, and of her, and all the time little moans of endearment mingled with the thrust of desire, rising and falling in a weird cacophony of sound that with each sigh brought fresh terror, until, suddenly, all was over. He rolled away from her, leaving her free.

And then suddenly she screamed.

Screamed and screamed.

There was a brief pause while he regained his breath and sat up, exhausted and alarmed.

She was already at the door of their room, less than half clad in a torn petticoat and bodice. He stumbled from the bed, pulled on his wrap and went after her, but it was too late. She'd reached the landing and stairs, and was still screaming.

'Come back,' Jon shouted, 'for God's sake – you little idiot Cass–'

But there was no pause in her wild flight; out she raced into the misty cold night – a zig-zag of blurred shape and whiteness that faded into a pin-point of thin cloud, then disappeared altogether.

Bemused and shocked Jon put a hand to his forehead and stood there briefly before turning to get a coat. At the same moment there was the sound of movement from the back of the building, and the housemaid appeared above on the landing.

'Mr Jon, sir, is anything the matter? Are you all right? We–'

Something in Jon's face silenced her.

He managed to control himself and say in rather harsh high tones, 'Your mistress has had a nightmare – we must – I must go after her – have hot drinks ready.'

Whether the girl did as he said he didn't know. Minutes later he'd pulled on boots and a mackintosh and with a torch was covering the grounds of Charnbrook following the direction of Cassie's disappearance. The Dower House stood not more than a quarter of a mile below the Hall practically on a level with the Lodge. The surrounding country was mostly parkland dotted with trees above a winding lane overlooking the forest.

The light was poor that night with a mere sliver of moon behind the thickening veil of cloud. Jon walked, head thrust forward, eyes scanning with difficulty every occasional lump of rock and tree trunk, calling at intervals, 'Cass – Cass' through a funnel formed by his hands. There was no response but the mournful distant crying of a night owl.

At last, just as he was about to cut down to the lane he glimpsed movement ahead and saw a humped shape gradually emerging from the distorted shadows – not a poacher which could have been expected – although poaching *could* have been his original mission at such an hour – but obviously some night wanderer who'd come across Cass. Her pale hair and white skirt trailed limply over his arms. Jon thought at first with a wild jerk of his heart she might be dead. The man was panting as he faced him.

Black hair straggled round his face which at close range could be seen to be dark, hawk-nosed and long, with the glint of gold in his ears.

A gypsy.

'This your lady, sir?' he asked, glancing down at his forlorn bundle. 'Lying there by that old stump she was.' He jerked a thumb over his shoulder. 'Had a fall. Glad to see you I am. Was wondering where to take her. Camping we are – near Fallow Wood. Then I thought of the big house. This is a fine Gorgio lady, I said to myself, like as not she belongs there.'

'Yes, yes–' Jon broke in. 'It's my wife. She'd had a shock – here let me take her.' He pulled Cassie to him and stared into her face. She moved slightly and opened her eyes, but there was no recognition in them, no response at all.

'I must get her back quickly,' he said, 'she's cold. I'm grateful to you. If you'd like to call tomorrow, at the Dower House – you may know it, the place below the Hall – I'll see you have something for your trouble.'

'No, sir. We Gagos – true Romanies – take

no benefit for giving a helping hand to a defenceless creature whether Gorgio, or our own kin. But take care, sir, she's not the kind to let wander the forest at night without reason or will.'

He touched his cap, turned and strode back into the mist.

Heavy-hearted, Jon carrying Cassandra, returned home, although he sensed it might not be his home for much longer.

Cassandra was lying on a couch by a fire in the lounge. She'd cringed and whimpered when Jon reached the foot of the stairs, still carrying her, so rugs and coverings had been fetched and an improvised bed arranged, with hot water bottles and a small table nearby holding a glass and decanter of brandy.

She let the spirit trickle through her lips down her throat, and a tinge of faint colour stained her white face. She appeared to be in no pain. There were no swollen ankles or apparent injury except a scratch on one wrist.

'In the morning,' Jon told the housekeeper

and maid, 'I shall call the doctor if necessary. I shan't require you any more tonight. So go and get your rest. And I'd be obliged if you kept quiet about this – this incident. Say nothing to anyone unless I give you leave.'

They agreed and returned to their own quarters.

For what seemed hours Cass lay with closed eyes seemingly unaware or uncaring of where she was or the abnormal circumstances of her being there.

Jon sat in a chair facing her on the opposite side of the fireplace, watching for any sign of recovery. But she remained static and expressionless as an effigy in marble lit at moments to fleeting pink when red and yellow flames leaped from the logs.

At intervals he got up and restlessly walked to the window, alternately blaming then justifying himself.

I didn't *harm* her, his mind insisted logically. It was only love. She knew that. She must have done. She didn't fight. Oh, God, Cass – what've we done to each other?

Sweat, mingled with unshed tears, trickled

from his forehead and eyes down the haggard creases of his face. As well as shocked he felt bewildered and angry at the same time. He was unable to envisage what the outcome might be. He'd thought at the beginning of their marriage that Cassie loved him. But if so it must have been a thin negative kind of emotion. Perhaps if she'd not read so many legends and got embroiled so deeply painting that nun she talked of – *if* she really existed – they could have got things right between them. They had certain interests in common, he appreciated decent art, and he still cared about her, but he knew he couldn't go on forever with her as she was.

Once during the night as he sat broodingly watching her, she opened her eyes and glanced at him through the firelight. He went to the sofa and bent down.

'Hullo, Cassie,' he said.

She stared at him, with a strange sweet smile on her lips, then lifted a hand. 'Do I know you?' she enquired.

Sick at heart, he answered, 'Of course, I'm your husband – Jon.'

She frowned faintly and echoed, 'Jon. Is that right? – Jon.'

'Yes. You had a shock. A nightmare. But it's over now. Don't worry. Go back to sleep. In the morning you'll remember.'

But if she did she didn't say so. She accepted him as her husband, but her manner was remote; it was rather as though they were meeting for the first time.

Once, when the pale morning sunlight caught his hair in a quivering ray from the window, she said, 'Your hair is so gold – like Launcelot's,' and he thought sadly, there seems nothing real about her any more. She's obsessed with her dreams. Heaven help us. How's it going to end?

When she'd had breakfast on a tray, however, she gradually changed and appeared more normal, although any reference to the evening's events was disregarded. Her only sign of distress appeared when Jon suggested she might like to go upstairs and have a wash and get dressed.

'No,' she said sharply. 'Not up there. I don't like this house. It has something sinister about it. Can't we go somewhere else to live – Jon? Somewhere new. I think there are – ghosts here, or something.'

Jon forced a laugh. 'Oh, rubbish. You've been listening to old stories. I know in the past superstitious people believed it was haunted. But that was simply because of its age. It's like a new home altogether now. Didn't you choose the decorations yourself? Remember? You wanted blue and gold with just a touch of crimson, and all white in the kitchen and upstairs. And you got what you wanted–'

She pressed her lips together in a small tight line. 'I don't like it any more. You say I had a nightmare. Nightmares aren't nice. I can't live here – I *can't*–'

The result was that after consultations with the doctor, the Wentworths and Emily and Walter Barrington, it was decided that it would be better for all concerned if Cassandra went to Beechlands immediately for a week or two to recover from whatever shock she'd had, while Jon somehow solved the problem of finding somewhere else to live.

No one except Jon knew the true reason of Cassandra's threatened breakdown. If she had recalled it, she never said.

Meanwhile Jon stayed temporarily at Charnbrook acting as bailiff, fulfilling many of the necessary duties concerning tenants' farms, and certain practical responsibilities at the stables.

Secretly Olivia was gratified to have her son under the same roof at Charnbrook, although she worried about the eventual outcome. She made an effort not to despise Cassandra; she was not entirely without feeling, and obviously Jon was still fond of his wife, but she found it hard to see any happy future for them.

'She's neurotic,' she insisted to her husband. 'Or perhaps it's just poor health, although the doctor didn't find anything wrong with her except a touch of anaemia. I suppose coming from her background made adjustment into a family like ours a strain sometimes. I know you think I could have behaved more kindly to her – but look how she behaved that night of the dinner party. Really, William!'

'I know. I know. We've got to wait, that's all. Don't want a scandal in the family if it can be helped. Maybe when the pair of them have had a bit of respite they'll get things into perspective and with luck have an heir! That's what's needed, y'know – a youngster to knock the stuffing out of all her airy-fairy painting business. But where are they going to live, eh?'

'I've been thinking,' Lady Wentworth said slowly, pondering, 'it would be possible surely to have a portion – one floor perhaps, of Charnbrook converted for their own living-quarters. We could then let the Dower House, furnished, for quite a large rent, to the right people of course. On a yearly lease, perhaps? We always seem to be short of funds these days, and this country's getting more and more popular with rich Americans, I'm told. In Boston especially they go for anything British.'

'You may have something there,' William agreed. 'It's quite an idea. Rick could be useful in getting contacts. He's embroiled at the moment with this wild project the Yanks have of putting moving picture stories on a screen. Can't believe it myself. But *he's* nobody's fool. Says it'll be a thriving industry in a few years.'

'He may well be right.'

'Could be – could be. Progress is a funny thing. You can never tell what's going to turn up next. Like the flying machine. There was talk, and experimenting, but very few people took the idea seriously. Then look what happened – The Wright Brothers did it for the States in 1903. Oh, they're a go-ahead lot, the Americans.'

There was a pause then he added thought-fully, 'We'll go into this business of letting the Dower House, Olivia. And I'll have a talk with Ferris about his newspaper – what's it called – *Pictorial* something? – maybe it would be worth taking up a few shares.'

'William, we've debts to pay first. I pray you'll be wise and think twice before you buy anything.'

Her husband gave a quirky smile. 'Some-times it's only by buying that you can pay off what you owe, my dear.'

She sighed. 'Oh. If only life was not so worrying. My first concern, and it should be yours, William, is somehow to see our son more happily settled.'

'It is, it is, and you needn't worry too much. There's one thing certain, whatever difficulties the boy has to face he'll come through all right in the end. He's a Wentworth.'

'How nice to be an optimist,' Olivia said a trifle sourly.

William gave her a shrewd look, and after a pause said, 'I'm going to have a talk with that man you took on to help in the greenhouse. It's my belief he hasn't a clue about tomatoes.'

Lady Wentworth opened her mouth to give a sharp retort, thought better of it, and the next moment her husband had left for the gardens.

Undue gossip between the domestic staff of the Dower House and Charnbrook Hall was avoided by retaining fees being paid to the former for a limited period, with the explanation that Mrs Wentworth junior had suffered a minor nervous breakdown which meant a temporary change of scene was necessary away from any domestic responsibilities.

Certain rumours, of course, were put about, but the nightmare theory seemed the most feasible, since Jon made almost daily visits to Beechlands, and appeared on friendly terms, and sincerely concerned about his wife.

Walter and Emily were naturally worried, though Cassandra herself, after the first few days, appeared content, and gradually settled into her former routine. She was always pleased to see Jon, and more than once told him it was like being engaged all over again. As the days passed faint wild-rose colour tinged her delicate face. From being over-thin, she put on a little weight, and when she smiled it was as though no dark memories lingered.

'I do love you so much, Jon,' she said, as she walked with him to the gate of the drive one evening. 'You know that, don't you?'

He studied her for a moment longing to take her in his arms, but not daring to. 'If you say so, Cass,' he said. 'One day–'

'Yes, yes,' she interrupted, 'one day we'll

be together for good – it's so romantic.'

His heart sank; it was like a cloud blotting out the sunlight. She was such a child. Either she didn't remember a thing or she was determined to live a fairytale existence of unreality, and he wondered how long he would be able to stand it, because her physical fascination for him remained. He still wanted her, but as a woman of flesh and blood. How could any man go on forever hungering after a dream when his body ached with normal physical desires?

At the end of March she started painting again, and set off in the mornings on her cycle for the Tree Studio.

Emily didn't entirely approve.

'I don't like you going off on your own so much,' she said to her one day, 'I've heard the gypsies are back.'

'I know. They're friendly people. They don't worry me,' Cassie answered, smiling. 'Didn't the doctor say I should feel free to go for walks and paint?'

'Yes, but your uncle and I are responsible for you – and to Jon. I can't believe he approves either.'

'Oh, he doesn't mind, not now,' Cassandra answered. 'We understand each other far better when we're apart, like this, just meeting when we feel like it.'

'And that's a very strange way to talk about your husband. Really, Cassandra! Sometimes I wonder if we did the right thing in having you back in this way.'

Cassie's large eyes widened. 'But I'm getting better, aren't I? And that's what they want, isn't it? The Wentworths?'

Emily could think of no satisfactory answer to the question, but when Cassandra had pedalled off along the lane that day on her cycle, she tackled Walter.

'I think you should write to your cousin,' she said, 'about Cassie.'

Walter looked up from his paper. 'Oh? You want her down here or something? Things not going right with the girl?'

'It depends on what you mean by right. She's happier. But you can't say things are normal between her and Jon.'

'Hm.'

'After all – living apart like this, because of a nightmare. Lots of folk have nightmares –

they don't let them break up a marriage, but if you ask me that's what's happening here. Now look here, Walter, face it, what do *we* know about the girl's background? Her *real* one? Did your cousin and her husband have all the details when they took her from that place, the orphanage, so long ago? Sometimes the authorities don't say, you know. But there's something that makes me uneasy about her nowadays. Something – secret and hidden – and strange, very strange.'

'Oh, come now–'

'No, you're not putting me off any longer. You *must* have the truth. Ask outright, *demand* it now we've got her on our hands. It's your duty, for all our sakes, including Cassandra's.'

Walter knew that his wife was right, and had a shrewd idea also that Ellen his cousin, and her husband, when he was living, had kept something they'd discovered about the girl's origins to themselves. Something unsavoury. However, he decided to keep the matter in abeyance for a bit before taking any definite action. The important thing to him seemed that the young couple still appeared fond of each other on the limited occasions they met, and the presence of Ellen Blacksley had always mildly irritated him – she was to his mind a boring 'do-gooder', and any question concerning the conduct of her adopted daughter would be sure to bring her down to Beechlands casting a shadow over the comfortable household routine.

Sensing his attitude, Emily did her best to let the problem rest temporarily, and concentrated her thoughts in the happier affairs of her own daughter and young children. She was sufficiently wise not to visit Woodgate more than once a week or fortnight, realizing that Rick – though always welcoming and pleasant if she arrived when he happened to be there – wouldn't appreciate too much intrusion by a mother-in-law. The important thing to Emily was that the couple seemed to be happy; Kate was blooming, and the twins were intriguing little things with completely different personalities. Marged, sturdy and strong-willed, already showed promise of developing into a dark-eyed beauty possessing Kate's charm and manner of getting what she wanted, Felicity on the other hand, was more shy, a dainty little creature, blue-eyed and more fair. The only worry concerning the babies was Felicity's health which had a tendency to mild chest trouble. But the doctors had assured their parents that in time she would almost certainly grow out of this one weakness.

Perhaps because he was not in the company of the babies as much as Kate, Rick appeared to be at rare times more doting than his wife. Emily privately considered that Kate was not sufficiently involved with the practical business of doing things for the children herself; and in a subtle way occasionally resented the compliments and attention lavished on them. 'A nurse – or a nanny as they call them these days *and* a maid fussing round all the time – it isn't the natural way of things,' she said to Walter. 'Kate sometimes seems to get irritable for no reason at all now. And then that housekeeper, Mrs Rook, all fuss and bustle acting as mistress more than someone employed to do a job. Why does Kate allow it? That's what I'd like to know.'

'She's been at Woodgate for a long time,' Walter pointed out. 'Now don't you start interfering, Emily, or popping over too much. Leave the family to go its own way.'

'I'm thinking of my *own* family,' Emily replied, ruffled. 'Our daughter, Kate.'

Actually, Kate had other things on her mind besides the children. She knew something was wrong between Jon and Cassandra, and was chagrined that she didn't know what. She didn't believe the simple explanation of a breakdown for one moment, and was determined somehow to discover the cause of the rift. Strangely, she was not only concerned on Jon's account, but experienced for the first time an odd kind of sympathy for Cass, recalling that when they were younger they'd had a few pleasant companionable times together, and there was something rather pathetic about the way she'd tried to make an impression at that awful wedding anniversary celebration – because that's all it had been surely – just a pitiful attempt to keep her end up against those snobby Wentworths? Or had Jon fallen out of love with her, was that it? Kate was surprised how little that possibility affected her: a few months, even weeks, ago she'd have felt a certain unkind triumph at the thought. But Rick's vitality, keeping pace with things, the birth of the twins, and all that life at Woodgate entailed had curtailed a good deal of her own romantic yearnings. Or perhaps she was maturing?– Oh, horrible thought. She'd certainly put on a *little* weight, she decided one afternoon, studying herself through the mirror. Even Rick, after viewing her appraisingly, had remarked teasingly, 'Don't worry about the pounds, darling, you're developing into a fine figure of a woman.'

She had been annoyed but had not shown it, deciding, however, that she must take more daily exercise. The twins didn't need her for much of the day, and the forest was at its loveliest for a wander now with bluebells thick among the ferns, and the trees lacy-pale in young green.

She determined from that moment to

make jaunts when convenient to the Tree Studio, and with luck find Cassie to learn what her reason was for leaving the Dower House.

So she set off one afternoon on foot, taking a rough track off the main lane, then making a short cut she knew well through the woods to the vicinity of the ruined priory and the nearby studio. The air was sweet and tangy. She discarded the light headscarf and let the gentle breeze ruffle her hair loosening a few bright copper curls. At one point there was a rustle overhead, and looking up she saw a red squirrel, bright-eyed, peering down at her. 'Hullo, you funny little thing,' she couldn't resist saying, much as she would have done as a child. 'What are you doing? Nothing?' There was a quick movement of the bushy tail, and it had lolloped down a branch and was gone.

Kate felt a kind of nostalgia. How carefree and happy those days had been, and what a joy it was to sense the old wonder and magic of the forest – alone for once, without the complex of secret longings and mixed emotions.

The Tree Studio was open when she arrived there, emerging like a fairytale place from its bed of tall bracken, flowering thorn and tangled undergrowth. Late primroses and dandelions like small suns starred the path leading to the door which was half open. Kate pushed through. 'Are you there, Cass?' She looked round. The familiar paint smell crept to meet her. Several pictures were propped up against the wall, landscapes and a few of animals including as she'd expected one or two portraits of the nun – with a larger one on the easel. It was a serene face, but full of subtle longing that Cass had captured in quite a masterly fashion. She's improved in her painting, Kate thought, she's really quite gifted. I wonder if Jon – Her thoughts broke off there, because she didn't quite know what she wondered about Jon these days. It was some time since she'd seen him.

She idled a few moments away indecisively, then went out again calling, 'Cass – Cass – I'm here, it's Kate. Are you around?' She paused, peering through the pale lacy pattern of bushes and interwoven brambles. There was no sign of Cassandra. So she took a thread of path winding through the wild spring jungle in the opposite direction from Beechlands. There was a green clearing quite near, and screwing up her eyes she saw the glimmer of water beyond. She'd been there many times always taking care not to venture too close; beautiful as it was – limpid and deep with a translucent shimmer on its clear surface – the soil round it was reputed to be slippery. They called it Old Harry's Pool because in the far past it was said a farmer and his horse had gone over and their drowned bodies never recovered. Originally it was one of the famous Burnwood slate pits.

For no logical feeling at all Kate felt a strange sensation of apprehension creep over her.

And then she saw her.

Cassie was standing only a few yards from the chasm. Through the fragile light her figure was a half-dimmed shape, and she appeared perfectly still – weirdly static – like an unmoving shape of the elements.

'Cass!' Kate called sharply. '*Cass* – what

are you doing there?' Cassandra turned. After a pause she swept her hair from her face, tossed it back over a shoulder, and came forward. She moved gracefully and, as she drew near, Kate saw she was smiling. She was wearing a long green embroidered skirt and a white high-necked blouse under a loose blue cape. The little cross falling from her neck on its silver chain glittered momentarily in a transient beam of thin sunlight.

'Hullo, Kate. I didn't expect you. I–' She paused before adding, 'I've just seen her.'

'Who?'

'The nun. She's beautiful, you know.'

Feeling vaguely shocked and irritated at the same time Kate said, 'Oh, Cass! how can you be *sure* she's a nun. There's no convent or women's priory round here any more. You must be wrong. Have you spoken to her?'

'No. But–'

'Well, then! Someone told me the other day there'd been an artist staying at that large farm near Bradgate for quite some time. I expect it's her. Artists do sometimes dress rather eccentrically. And apparently she does a lot of walking up the Beacon and round the forest.'

'*I know* she's a nun,' Cassandra persisted. 'Think what you like. Why does everyone doubt my word?'

Kate sighed. 'Oh, well, have it your way. I suppose it doesn't matter. If you want to believe she's a nun, that's it. But Jon must think it pretty odd.'

'Jon? Why should he? Anyway, he doesn't pry into who I meet. He's interested in my painting. He always was.'

'Is he? And what about your marriage?'

'Well, what about it? We're happy, if that's what you want to know.'

'Then why on earth don't you go back to the Dower House?'

Cassandra's colour faded leaving only two brilliant spots of scarlet on her cheek-bones when she stopped suddenly and faced her cousin tight-lipped with her eyes wide and staring, both hands clenched. 'Because I *hate* that place – *hate* it, and you've no right to upset me. The doctor said I should have peace.'

Kate tried to pacify her. 'I'm sorry, I didn't mean to worry you. I was wrong to say anything. But it seems so strange.'

'That's because you're married to Rick. If it was Jon you'd understand – he's very sensitive; we're not like you two.'

'No, you're certainly not,' Kate remarked with a touch of acerbity, and had a mental picture of Rick's reaction should she behave like Cass.

There was silence for some moments as the girls turned into the path to the Studio. By the time they got there Cass's angry mood had passed, and she appeared contrite.

'It was nice of you to come really,' she said. 'I'm sorry about my temper. It's so important to keep serene – whatever happens.'

Her words, and the soft manner she spoke them, for some unpredictable reason sent a little shiver down Kate's spine.

'I'll come again, unless you'd rather I didn't.'

'No of course I don't mind. It's nice seeing you, so long as we don't argue.'

Kate forced a smile. 'I'll do my best. Now,

can I look at your most recent paintings?'

'They're over there.' Cass pointed to a corner. 'The new portraits, the one on the easel, isn't finished yet.'

Close inspection of the watercolours revealed beside delicate detail, surprising suggestions of hidden faces and forms, which although only vaguely defined – probably because of that – were proof of Cassandra's extraordinary imagination. This of course was at the root of the nun business, Kate told herself on the way back to Beechlands. Cass must realize herself surely that the demure face of the gentle woman in the painting was either a creation of her own mind, or of someone she'd met on her rambles and used as a subject.

Kate intended to take a second walk to the Studio the following week, but was diverted by a dramatic upheaval that put all other matters temporarily out of her mind.

Rick informed her one evening that he had a friend coming for the evening meal the following day – a Richard Owen from Wales.

'So tell Mrs Rook to see Cook has something tasty for the meal – tasty but straightforward without frills,' he said. 'I'll arrange the wine. It's quite an occasion. We've decided to take a trip together to the States about April. Maybe he'll take up shares in the *Review*, and his mining interests over there. So do your best to put on a good show, darling.'

Kate stared at him. She was looking particularly lovely in shimmering sea-green with just a faint shadowed suggestion of the cream bosom beneath the low-cut silk of the bodice.

'*What* did you say? A *trip*? To America, do you mean?'

He glanced at her warily. 'That's right. Business purely. It won't be for long, eight days each way on the water and a week or so there. No more than a month altogether.'

'But—' She broke off, her mind whirling, then continued, only half believing what she'd heard, 'Do you mean without me?'

He put on his most placating smile, and took her hand. 'Oh, come now, sweetheart. What would you do on your own over there, knowing nobody, no woman to talk to—'

'Not even Mrs Linda Wade?' The question

was out before she knew it.

His face darkened slightly. 'Now Kate, I thought we'd settled the place of Mrs Wade in our routine. No questions, no petty jealous ideas – don't start creating a scene at this stage of our marriage. No, as far as I know, Mrs Wade will *not* be on the *Oceanic* when we sail. If she is it will be through no suggestion of mine. As I've just pointed out it will be an all-male business trip.'

'But you're always having business trips to somewhere or other, London or Wales, and – and all over the place. And I never go *any*where – never – Rick.' Her voice softened, became pleading, she looking up at him with her large eyes limpid and pleading. 'Please, oh *please, do* let me come. I wouldn't be in the way. If you love me–'

He studied her seriously. 'I *do* love you Kate. Much much more than you realize. But it's really not convenient or suitable to have you with me this time. Another thing – and this is *most* important: there are the twins. I wouldn't want them to be left entirely to the care of servants for *four* weeks. Felicity isn't a strong child and needs a mother at hand in case of any problem. You must see that. Don't you?'

He took her hand. She pulled it away sharply. 'Yes, I see. Oh, I see. You're using me. You *always* use me, and give me nothing in return.'

She put a hand to her mouth, aghast at her outburst. He put both hands on her arms, gave her a quick shake and forced her to look at him.

'So I *use* you, do I? – and give you nothing. What about this?' He indicated the rich exotic interior. 'The endless hours I've spent pandering to your whims and wishes – in spite of your secret lusting for fancy words and God knows what else from your fair-haired Galahad. Nothing?'

'I didn't mean that. It was just – frustration.'

His mouth tightened. 'Then I advise you, Mrs Ferris, to try curbing your frustrations, and concentrate on your manners, or I may have to resort to my own methods of controlling a wilful wife.'

She bit her lip, released herself, and walked to the window. Her handkerchief became a small ball in her hand. Why couldn't he understand? But he seemed able to take everything so lightly – to make a decision, and it was *fait accompli* – done. The clash of words had shaken her. Her throat was tight with emotion. She struggled for composure, and was steeling herself to appear calm and uncaring when he came up behind her. She sensed rather than heard his presence there with a shock of awareness almost electric.

Firmly he turned her round and stared into her face, looking deep into her eyes. A glisten of unshed tears glittered on the thick velvet lashes, spreading gradually into tormented pools of darkness.

'Oh, Kate,' he said, 'what am I to do with you? Spank you, or love you?'

He shook his head slowly, then gently at first his lips were on hers, and her arms were reaching to his shoulders.

That moment held a wonder and magic that was completely new to her. It was then that she first knew, without admitting it, that she loved him.

At the end of March he went to America.

5

Kate did her best not to show distress at Rick's departure, knowing the granite streak in his character would not appreciate any undue display of unnecessary emotion. For him the brief four weeks would be an occasion of exhilarating business contacts needing all his concentrated expertise in assessing lucrative financial possibilities.

The adventurer had been stirred by the vision of subtle mental duelling ahead. Whatever line he took, in whatever project, he meant to be on the winning side. The world was quickly changing; Britain still remained the great industrial power, but in the United States were the seeds of the New World, and if possible he meant to be a step ahead in both.

He could not think of Kate without a rush of longing in his heart and loins, so he did not think of her overmuch. But with Kate it was quite different.

She resented the abrupt parting, and the fact that he could, with such apparent blitheness, sail away leaving her at Woodgate with a house of dull female servants except for the one man, and two uncompanionable babies who were generally asleep or wailing and wanting to be fed or carried round the room in the arms of the nanny whenever she approached.

She told herself constantly she loved them, and she did, on the rare occasions when they were quiet and could even smile like beaming cherubs of fiction. But because her time with them was so severely monitored by the nurse or the maid, she had little chance of really getting to know them.

Once or twice she took them in the carriage to Beechlands, but on each time Felicity had wind and, despite Emily's protests, on the insistence of Nanny Green, they returned after only an hour to Woodgate.

The truth was, Kate decided, her own presence with the children seemed to be superfluous. Perhaps when they were older she would feel differently, but it had been quite ridiculous of Rick to make the babies an excuse for leaving her behind. Strangely, since her marriage, she had got to know few local people. Most were either too old or too immature to be interested in a young mother. The rest either belonged to the select little hunting crowd with whom she had nothing in common, or to the few shopkeepers in the village whose limited means kept them aloof from being on familiar terms with the wealthy Mrs Rick Ferris. The farming fraternity came nearest in any possible companionship. But they were always too busy, and anyway, Kate thought, you couldn't call farmers' wives exactly stimulating conversationally, and she hated thinking of animals being killed, or being made to realize that a playful cuddly young lamb seen playing in a field one day might be served up on a dinner plate the following week.

So her only real diversions during that period were as they had been before her marriage – shopping sprees.

She ordered a new outfit to be made by a

dressmaker in Lynchester. It was to be a costume of deep blue silk with a fitted waist meant to win admiration and approval from Rick when he returned from America. She had not forgotten his comment of 'a fine figure of a woman', and was already dieting in a mild amateurish way.

She also kept to her determination for regular physical activity every day, and when she felt in the mood went over to see Cass in her Studio.

There were several different routes from Woodgate to the site, one leading half-way down a lane bordering the encampments used by gypsies on their travels between Larchborough and Lynchester.

On a fine late April morning following her short daily session with the twins – just twenty minutes which was considered ample time by both Nanny and Mrs Rook – Kate set off in this direction wearing light boots and a loose yellow cape over a rust-coloured dress patterned with small white daisies. Her curiosity concerning the rift between her cousin and Jon had in no way abated, but rather increased in Rick's absence. So she was a little nonplussed and frustrated to arrive there after a two-mile walk to find Jon present. Cass was looking vaguely troubled, and Jon, she thought, more gaunt than when she'd last seen him.

'Oh, hullo,' she remarked rather lamely. 'I hope I'm not intruding. Don't worry though, I'm not staying. I do a good deal of walking these days.' There was a short pause, 'for my figure you know.' She nodded with an attempt at lightness.

Jon managed a humourless smile. 'Ah! – the young matron à la mode.' His gaze studied Kate's form through tired, heavy-lidded eyes. 'A pity you can't wave a magic wand and give Cassandra a few pounds.'

'There's no need to be personal,' Kate said sharply. 'I'm off again anyway. I'll look in another day, Cass.' She turned and was out of the door again when Jon sprang forward, pushed by and stopped her. 'Oh, don't be so touchy. I was leaving when you appeared like a warm breath of air in an icy atmosphere. For Pete's sake try and cheer Cass up. I've done my best, but as usual it's landed me in the dog-house.' He pulled a cap from a pocket of his jacket and slammed it on his head.

'Bye-ee. Nice to see you looking so gorgeous.' The next moment he was off down the path, and had turned a corner into the lane.

With feelings bordering between reluctance and irritation Kate turned and joined Cassandra.

'What's the matter with Jon today?' Kate said. 'Or was it just that he was annoyed at being interrupted?'

'No, not that,' Cassandra answered. 'He gets moods sometimes, so do I.'

'No wonder really,' Kate remarked tactlessly. 'It's such an odd life you two lead.' When Cassandra remained silent, she continued in cautious wheedling tones, 'Can't you tell me all about it. Cass, what happened that night – the night you had the dream – or whatever it was? Perhaps you'd feel better. It does help sometimes, having someone to confide in when you have a problem.'

'I've no problem,' Cass told her coldly. 'I'm just – frustrated. She generally comes to the pool, in the early afternoons. I'm trying to finish that portrait, but she hasn't turned up today, and I'll have to get back to Beechlands soon or Aunt Emily will make a fuss.'

'You're talking about your – about the nun, I suppose?'

'Who else? I've no other model.'

'You could have though – there are squirrels and deer, and–'

'I don't *want* squirrels and deer. I want her, and I wish you wouldn't interfere. Jon was like that before you came today. He's always *wanting*. He wants this – he wants that – never what *I* want–'

Kate stifled the desire to make an angry comment and said gently, 'Well, Cass, perhaps it's natural. He loves you; don't forget that. And I thought it was the same with you.'

'It *was,* and *is.* I do love Jon. But–' All vitality appeared to drain from her suddenly. She looked tired and exhausted, almost ill. 'I'm sorry,' she said. 'I feel so lost sometimes – lonely; and yet I have to be alone, because–' Her voice faltered. 'Oh, you couldn't possibly understand. I don't always understand myself. But I *do* know that when I've finished the painting things will be better. They must be. Or–'

'Yes? Or–?'

'Oh, I don't know. Forget this stupid conversation, Kate. I'll have to be getting back presently. Are you going my way?'

'No, it would be a long way round. But we can go down the lane together. Have you got your cycle?'

'Yes, it's at the back.'

'All right then. Whenever you're ready.'

Five minutes later the Studio door was safely shut, and the two of them were walking down the lane with Cassandra pushing her bicycle. They parted at the point where the path wound from the lane through the trees towards Woodgate, and as she watched Cassandra pedal down the winding stretch of roadway leading towards Beechlands, Kate noticed the glimmer of red and gold vehicles through the interlaced branches of chestnut trees.

So the gypsies were back.

She hoped Cassandra wouldn't get too

involved with them, although a diversion to take her mind off the supposed nun for a bit might be beneficial.

She only saw her cousin twice more during the following fortnight. On the first occasion Cassandra appeared unusually happy and lighthearted; she'd finished the portrait which was quite compelling in a thoughtful ethereal way, Kate thought. Cass's attitude to Jon was very different from the last time they'd met. He'd become her legendary heroic lover again.

'Darling Jon,' she sighed, when Kate enquired after him. 'He's only just left. We *are* so terribly in love, you know. Just fancy! He kissed my hand today, and called me his 'fairy child' and 'princess' – imagine it. Isn't it wonderful?'

Yes, Kate could *imagine* it. But she didn't believe it for one moment, and she found the sentiment slightly ridiculous, and rather frightening. What was happening to Cass? What *had* happened? Was she losing her reason?

The thought worried her, with the result that a week later – a week before Rick's return from America, she made another visit to the Studio.

This time it was quite different.

Cass was not there.

It was a still afternoon with a thin yellowish sky and a faint ground mist, more like autumn than spring. But the earth held a sweet tangy odour suggestive of young growing things.

Everything was very quiet. From the distance, mingled with the occasional chirp of a bird came the rise and fall of gypsy music – of violins that faded as Kate stood listening.

'Are you there, Cass?' she called moving to the Studio entrance. There was no reply. She pushed the half-open door wider and stared.

The interior was a jumble. Canvasses and paintings lay strewn about the floor; Cass's blue cloak lay over a chair, a stream of golden liquid trickled from a small bottle in a corner, and at the far end a figure was slouched into a lump surrounded by pieces of a slashed painting – the portrait.

Aghast, Kate went in, and the figure

moved, staggering to its feet.

Jon.

A Jon distraught and angry-looking, with a shining large penknife in his hand. His fair hair had fallen over one eye. Kate thought at first he was drunk. Then he spoke. His voice was throaty with exhaustion, but cold and calculating, holding a frightening finality in it.

'So it's you,' he said. 'Well, as you see, I've done it. Done it at last. Destroyed the wretched thing.' He put a hand to his head. 'For God's sake sit down or do something. Speak, can't you – tell me off in any bloody way you like – but move, speak – don't just stand there.'

He staggered slightly; Kate went towards him.

'Oh, Jon.'

'That's right – Jon, Jon, the noble squire's wicked son – destroyer of pictures and seducer of women. But then that wouldn't be true, would it? Cassandra's unseducable, and you, Kate – what about you?'

He lurched and almost fell. Kate put out an arm and steadied him.

'Sit down,' she heard herself saying as firmly and quietly as possible. 'Rest a bit, and then – tell me about it, and get it off your chest. What's happened? Where's Cass?'

He flung himself on to the divan and sat there with his head in his hands before facing her.

'I've no idea where Cass is,' he answered. 'I've waited and waited for hours but there's no sign of her – only that damned nun creature and that's gone for good now, hasn't it? *Hasn't* it?'

'Yes, yes. I suppose so,' Kate answered gently.

'You suppose? Ah, well! Yes – I guess that's all anyone *can* do about Cass and her – obsession. Just wonder.'

For a moment his expression changed and was solemn, holding a great sadness in his blue eyes when he continued, 'It's killing us both, you know. And for what reason? What does she get out of it all? It's only pretence, you know – imagination – this thing about the nun. I've made enquiries from everyone around here, and no one else has seen or heard of her. Maybe she exists in that big book on the floor there below the cupboard – I don't know. I've intended to tear it up, get rid of it. But now – now that holier-than-thou face has gone perhaps there's no need.'

'No, I'd leave it,' Kate said quietly. 'You don't know whose book it is; it could be your father's and valuable. But the portrait! Would it be best do you think to pack it right away somewhere, perhaps bury it or throw it in the pool? Then if we tidied up the place and both left before Cass came – or anyone – it could look as though someone had just come in and stolen it. If Cass knew the truth there's sure to be an awful scene and all sorts of enquiries. You don't want that, do you?'

'God, no. I only want one thing. I only ever did, since I first saw her. I want Cass back. Cass as she was at Isabella's dance wearing the dress you lent her.'

Pity stirred Kate to say gently, 'Jon, I'm so sorry. So truly sorry; I'd do anything I could to help but–!' Her voice faltered as she recognized with bewilderment the sudden hope spring into Jon's eyes bringing youth back briefly to the handsome worn-out countenance.

'You would, Kate? Really?' He got up, went towards her, and took both her hands in his. At first she did not resist. He was the Jon she remembered. 'You always liked me, didn't you?' he said huskily, drawing her close. 'We liked each other. You were always so – so bright and warm.'

She trembled, torn by a strange mixed sensation of fear, pity, and memories of the past. A hand sought the softness of a breast. She recalled Rick with shock.

'Let me go,' she said, feeling Jon's hot breath against her cheek. 'Jon – we mustn't.' She struggled to free herself. 'I didn't mean – *Jon*!' He was pressing his mouth against her neck and lips, smothering her protests, while her body arched back under the weight of his, almost forcing her to the floor. Then suddenly there was the creaking of the door, a shadow of the light, and he freed her. But not before a woman's high, light voice cried shrilly, 'Don't stop because of me.'

Both turned to see Cassie's silhouetted

figure standing rigidly at the entrance.

Kate couldn't speak for a moment; she was aware only of shock, of Jon's figure standing like a block of frozen wood beside her, and as Cassandra swept in – of a blazing white face and contemptuous staring eyes. Then in a rush of words the power of speech returned, and with it movement. Kate rushed forward, 'Cassie it's not what you think – it's nothing, you must believe it – Jon was just needing you, and I was here. It's all a terrible muddle – a mistake – listen–'

'I don't care if it was a mistake or not. I don't care what you do, either of you. But–' For the first time Cassandra appeared to notice the slashed and torn portrait on the floor. She knelt down and lifted up the pieces of canvas, examining each with a kind of numbed despair. Then she lifted her head and stared at Kate accusingly. 'You did this. *You* – you've wilfully spoiled all I've worked for – all I cared about–'

'*No,*' Jon interrupted harshly. '*I* did it and good riddance. Now shut up, put on your cape and come back with me like a sane human being, or – or – God knows what'll become of us.' He turned away and stood leaning at the door, head down, his face covered by one hand, a forlorn, deflated figure. At that moment Kate didn't know which was the most to be pitied – Jon or Cass.

She bent and touched the other girl's shoulder. 'Cass try and forget all this. It was just – unhappiness. I know what it must look like to you – and I'm sorry about the painting. But–'

Cass gave her a fleeting glance. Her expression was bleak, controlled by an icy veneer covering inner despair and confusion. 'I've said it doesn't matter – not you or him,' Cass retorted. 'So don't – don't talk. I'm going–' Jon glanced up hopefully, 'back to Beechlands,' Cass concluded, 'when I've collected all this.' She started picking up the remaining bits of the painting, trying to piece them together. Then she placed them helplessly on a chair and reached for her cape. After she got to her feet Kate saw the blur of tears in her eyes.

'If you're going now I'm coming with you. You're not leaving in this state.'

In spite of her distress Cassandra managed an icy tight little smile, false but with a hint of triumph in it. 'You're not. I've got my bicycle. So, do you mind leaving, both of you? I don't want people prying and poking round. I want the door properly shut.'

Knowing that only force could stop her they had to do as she said, and a few minutes later Kate and Jon parted to go their different ways.

'I wish I'd never come today,' Kate said bitterly before she took the path through the woods leading to Woodgate. 'Oh, how I wish I hadn't.'

Jon gave her a shrewd bitter glance and retorted. 'But you did, didn't you? I wonder why?'

Then he turned and walked away apparently recovered, with a jaunty air and swagger that she knew nevertheless was pretence.

A deep unhappiness flooded her. She sensed the day might have repercussions none of them as yet could envisage, and the awareness held an odd feeling of mounting apprehension that was almost fear.

Cassandra left for the forest early the next day, in spite of Emily's protests.

'You look a bit "wisht" dear, tired,' she said. 'Aren't you working too much at your painting these days? What about taking a little trip into Lynchester? We could do a bit of shopping and perhaps have a light meal at that nice place near the Market Place?'

Cassandra shook her head. 'No, I'm sorry, I don't feel like shops and crowds, and–'

'There won't be crowds today. There's no market on Wednesdays, we could–'

'No, *really.*' Cass's voice was stubborn. 'I have things to do at the Studio. Tidying up, and finishing something. I thought I'd take sandwiches and come back later. *Please.* Don't try and press me. There's no shopping I want to do anyway. It would be a waste of time.'

Emily was forced to agree in the end, and shortly after their brief conversation Cass set off on her cycle with a packet of hastily prepared food hanging in a bag from her handlebars.

There was no wind at all that morning, everything was very still, almost unnaturally so. A faint shroud of mist filmed undergrowth and trees, glistening at moments from shafts of pale sunlight silvering the spring green.

She'll be there today, Cass thought. She's sure to be. And a deep spreading sense of contentment flooded through her, dispelling the distress and ugliness of the previous afternoon. Quite what she intended to do she didn't know. The portrait was gone, and she'd no intention of trying to repeat it. All through the night hours when she'd hardly slept, her mind had been a jargon of unformed thoughts and depression that had affected her whole body making her rigid with pain – pain not caused primarily by Kate, but from Jon's betrayal, and once more that dark risen thing from the past that was always waiting to assume its identity of terror.

The latter was worst of all.

As she unfastened the door of the Studio

a deep menacing melancholy seemed to hover there from the shadowed walls, empty easel, and still a few scattered remains of the portrait.

I must have a glass of my tonic, she thought, then I'll feel better.

She went to the small cupboard where an odd mixture of articles were stored – a few paints, and a row of bottles on a shelf containing various potions mixed from herbs and other simple ingredients suggested in the old-fashioned book which contained as well, recipes for wines, and certain spells used in ancient times for stimulating love for the heart-sick.

Cassandra had bought it all, during the past year, from a roving pedlar who had discovered her one day in her forest retreat. He was one on his own – a 'mumper', half-bred gypsy whom the true Romanies camping with the *vardos* and horses in Burnwood would have nothing to do with. But he had captivated Cassandra's interest with his wily tongue and ways, and quite soon after his first visit she'd tried a sip of the golden liquid in one of the bottles. It had appeared to do her no harm; the taste savoured slightly of elderflower, although she had not recognized it, and after the first few sips a happy sense of elation had possessed her. It was tonic indeed, dispelling the fits of strange depression that had threatened her at times since childhood.

She'd told no one, of course, and since her marriage to Jon had been more careful than ever to keep the medicine or 'tonic' as she called it hidden away. At the present time she had only three small bottles left, but soon, when the summer fairs were winding through the countryside, she knew the old 'mumper', in his long, black, flapping coat with wizened face and bedraggled hair under his squashed-down top-hat, would be around and call on her. She would be ready with money to pay him well, after which he'd mutter some sort of foreign blessing and be gone, fleet as a sly old fox disappearing through the trees.

He knew by keen watchfulness and an uncanny instinct when the Gorgio lady would be alone, and how to avoid detection from others.

The gypsies hated him and would have harmed him, if they hadn't taken such care to cause no trouble with the police or with the natives, especially the gentry, and farming folk of the district.

So the understanding between the Gorgio lady and the despised and cunning mumper had continued and on that certain summer's day following Cassandra's upsetting encounter with Jon and Kate, she was more than ever grateful for the insidious help offered by his liquid concoction.

She took three good sips, and in no more than half a minute felt the familiar sense of well-being spread through her veins and nerves. Her intuitive sense that told her the gentle figure – the wanderer of the forest who had been her model and secret companion for so many months – would be there that day, intensified to certainty.

The weather was already mild and dewy bright as she took off her cape, laid it over the chair and set off along the familiar thin path to the place that had become for her a sanctuary.

In a few minutes she had reached a point

where the glitter of the ancient pool was visible. There was no stirring of air through the undergrowth, only the transient light of lifting sun and shade patterning the massed slender trunks of birch and oak.

Feeling the morning's sweetness on her face, Cassandra lifted her head, and shook her long pale hair free.

She stared intently through the tracery of branches, and then she saw her – a static shape swathed in draperies with arms outstretched as though to embrace the iridescent sky.

Cass held her breath.

It was as though communion flowed between them. There was no darkness any more – no constant inner battle to forget – *forget*. Because the 'thing' she'd always had to live with unconsciously was no longer there. All was purified and clean.

Her whole body relaxed, and with it the form near the waiting pool moved slowly, gracefully, in an aura of strange peace, one hand extended as though in welcome.

In a second of time, the face looking towards Cassandra was sweetly smiling, beatific. Then the long robes became a mere shadow on the green surface of the pool before the water claimed it and it was gone.

In a daze, but still strangely elated, Cassandra pushed her way through the undergrowth. This was the end, she knew, and also the beginning. There would be no more Jon – no more earthly presence claiming what she could not give.

Very deliberately she stepped over the bordering rocks and rough earth, and fell.

There was a splash as her body hit the water, a faint gurgling sound, followed by the flutter and crying of a lone bird.

Then silence.

It was not until late afternoon she was found, her long skirt caught on a jagged spike of rock which had prevented her completely sinking. Nothing of her body was visible except one small white hand reaching through the clear green like a waterlily opening to the sunlight.

One of the gypsies out gathering wood and on the watch probably for a rabbit, had first spotted an unusual reflected shape immersed in the pool. He'd returned to the camp immediately, untethered one of the horses and ridden to the nearest large house which happened to be Beechlands. It was already late afternoon, and Emily was getting worried as Cassandra had not returned from her day's painting. She instantly called Walter from the study and he got in touch with the police. By the time they'd arrived dusk was falling, and the day's faint mist turning to fog; so activity had had to be suspended until the following day. Meanwhile a message was got through to Jon who was present when the bedraggled corpse of his wife was eventually recovered.

'That's her,' he said to a police officer, 'that's Cassandra.' His voice was hard, without emotion, his face bleak and expressionless.

'Your wife, sir?'

'Yes. You could call her that. We were married – in church – if that's what you want to know.'

He walked away before the sheet was put over the dead face, got into the waiting chaise and drove back to Charnbrook.

An autopsy revealed only a slight amount of alcohol in Cass's stomach which could not have been responsible for her death and was possibly that of a certain amount of the herbal brew found by the police in the Studio. At the following inquest a verdict of Accidental Death from drowning was recorded. It was thought the girl had gone for a walk in the mist, wandered mistakenly from the footpath, lost her footing, and fallen into the ancient slate pit. The adjoining ground was common land, but directions were given to county authorities to have that certain patch of ground safely sealed off to prevent further accidents of a similar nature.

At the beginning of the official proceedings the gypsies had been interviewed concerning their knowledge of the habits of the tragic young wife, including questions concerning the non-poisonous but insidious herbal wines in her possession. Had she brewed them herself? Or possibly obtained them from the travellers?

All had denied any such connection. They were Romanies. They kept to themselves. They would have no such dealings with Gorgio fine ladies from big houses. Only one – an ancient crone, Sarah Boswell, let out that the poor young *rawni* had met her one day by chance when she was out mushrooming, and had tried to get a cure from her; she thought she was with *chavi*, and didn't want the baby. But she'd refused. They were a law-abiding tribe – the Boswells, and didn't want the *gavvers* on their track. To act in such a way would be *mochardi* – unclean and against the law of O Del.

There was no sign medically that Cassandra was pregnant or ever had been, and the police had let the matter rest there, leaving the old woman muttering to herself.

Cassandra's funeral was held shortly following Rick's return from the States. It was a sad quiet occasion, with only the Barringtons, Wentworths, Ferrises and Ellen Blacksley present. Jon's and Kate's eyes met once before she was laid to rest in the family vault at Charnbrook. The glance from Jon was direct, cold, yet enigmatic. What he was trying to convey Kate did not know. But a shiver momentarily stiffened her spine, and she wanted only one thing – for the morbid occasion to be over and herself back at Woodgate with Rick's arms comfortingly round her.

6

Cassandra's tragic end and the events immediately following, had a subtle but sobering effect on what should have been a joyful period for Kate and Rick after his sojourn in America. Their lovemaking was as intense as ever; whenever he appeared in a doorway, passed on the stairs, or was in any close proximity, her whole being became momentarily electrified. His touch set her body and nerves on fire. She hadn't realized completely before how vital and necessary his presence had become in her life. And yet, a faint shadow was apt to cloud her spirits in periods when she was on her own – the memory of Jon's gaze at the funeral – something hard and unforgiving – of what, she didn't know – a condemnation that was like a mental sword thrust, blaming her.

For what?

And why?

She began to sleep badly, and one morning early, when Rick had departed for his offices in Lynchester, she called to see the local doctor in Woodgate who, making an examination, after taking details of her vague aches and pains and slight nausea, told her with a smile that in his opinion, although at an early stage, he was as certain as he could be that she was once more pregnant.

Kate left the surgery in a daze. Such a possibility had simply not occurred to her, overshadowed as the past two months had been by Rick's departure, and all the other problems concerning Jon and Cassandra. But when she counted up the weeks combined with certain physical signs that hadn't seemed important at the time she recognized that the doctor's diagnosis was not only possible but probably quite right.

The night before Rick left, had been one of intensified passion between them.

But – another baby! So near the twins.

Three children in two years!

The idea made her mind boggle.

Still, she told herself optimistically, Rick would probably be pleased. She'd always felt that however much he loved Marged and Felicity, he'd secretly hoped for a son. So perhaps this time his wish would be granted.

As she'd anticipated, her husband was elated when she told him that evening as she sat brushing her hair at the dressing-table. She was wearing a lacy wrap over a chiffon embroidered nightdress that had flowing bell-shaped sleeves and a flimsy collar tied at the neck with a bow.

He came through from the dressing-room in his wrap over a long nightshirt, went to the back of her chair, stooped, put a hand round each breast and planted a kiss on her neck.

'You look so beautiful,' he said softly. 'My lovely wife.'

'And "a fine figure of a woman",' she remarked teasingly. 'That's what you said before.'

'I should have been shot for being so unchivalrous.'

She stared up at him, smiling. 'But it's true

– or *will* be presently–' She broke off.

He knitted his eyes together. '*Presently? What does that mean?*'

'I saw the doctor today, and I'm having another baby, Rick, in about six – or seven months. I'm not *quite* sure of the date, but it must have happened that night before you went away to America. Remember?'

He stared at her and smiled with a look almost of wonder on his face she'd never seen before, and before she quite knew what was happening, he'd lifted her up and was holding her close, with his lips on hers. She smelt sweet and rich, he thought, like a rose from the garden, and her luxurious russet hair rippled over his left arm like a silken cloak.

'Oh, Kate,' he murmured, 'how lucky we are. This news is a hundred times more precious than all the deals I've made in America.'

'I should just think so, and don't you dare compare me with any commercial deal,' she cried. 'Having a baby's no fun, you know.'

'I *don't* know, but I'll take your word for it.'

She sighed happily. 'I hope it's a boy.'

'It would be rather gratifying, but if it's not – there's still plenty of time.'

'You're insatiable.'

'Yes – where you're concerned.'

And so the evening passed, filled with endearments and plans and promises without either of them contemplating that fate might hold a hidden card of its own to play in their destiny.

For the present Rick and Kate decided to keep their news of Kate's condition to themselves, feeling that on top of Cassandra's death any show of celebration might appear hurtful and out of taste to Ellen Blacksley who stayed on at Beechlands for a short time following the funeral.

She was a practical, stolid type of woman with, nevertheless, a certain sensitivity that she'd struggled successfully, so far, to hide under a brave veneer of common-sense. And she had been genuinely fond of her adopted daughter.

Emily recognized, without bringing the hurtful topic up that she had something to discuss or impart about Cassandra, and on the evening of her departure for the North the next day, it came out.

The three of them, Ellen, Emily and Walter, were seated in the large lounge after dinner with the fading early summer light slanting through the french windows across the tasteful, rather old-fashioned but luxurious, interior. Walter was about to retire to the billiard-room for a smoke, then take an evening stroll out with his dogs, Sam, an Irish terrier, and Joe, the bulldog.

'No, don't go, Walter,' Ellen said, as he got up from his chair. 'Not yet for a bit. I've something to say to you about Cassandra.'

'Oh?' Walter returned to his chair. 'That's all right then. What is it? Emily and I will be grateful to hear anything you've got on your mind. It's been a tragic time for you, especially after all you've done for the girl – you and Wilf. It was through Wilf that you first got to hear of her, of course, or should I say his work as a man of God?' He cleared his throat. 'No matter. Speak, love. We've often wondered about her.'

Ellen was quiet for a moment, then she said, 'Yes, you must have. In the ordinary way, when a young child's adopted, not much is said of its background to the new parents. But with Cassie it was different. If it hadn't been for Wilf being a minister nothing to this day might've come out. and Wilf and I wouldn't have heard of her. But the poor little thing.' There was a pause before she continued. 'She was only four, you know, when my husband came upon her in that orphanage place. She was sick at that time – not physically, or exactly deranged, but in a kind of shock. She hadn't spoken or communicated in any proper way for months since it – it happened.'

In the short silence that followed only the buzzing of a bee could be heard as it flew through the half-open window and out again. Then Emily said gently, 'Go on, dear. Tell us. After what?'

'The murder,' Ellen said bluntly. 'Cassie's mother was murdered by her second husband, Cassie's stepfather, and the child witnessed it all. She was *there*.'

'Oh,' Emily gave a little gasp. 'How dreadful.'

'Yes. When they broke in – neighbours had

heard screams and got the police – the child, little more than a baby – was just standing staring at her mother lying in a pool of blood. The husband, a large brute of a man, had come home drunk that night and there'd been a row of some sort. He'd violated his wife first then stabbed her with a kitchen knife. He was lolling half senseless in a chair, quite naked. Oh, it was in all the papers at the time. He was tried later, and sentenced to death, of course, but died of a stroke before the sentence was carried out. To the public the story ended there. The little girl was taken to hospital first, then after a time to the home where Wilf visited. That's how we came by her. Her true name and identity had been kept secret from everyone but the doctors and one or two officials and, of course, Wilf, being a trusted and devout Christian.' Ellen hesitated, then continued, 'That's the way it was. *You* know, Walter, how Wilf and I'd wanted a child, and how, somehow, it hadn't come about – well, when this awful thing happened Wilf saw the hand of God pointing our way, and we adopted her as ours, signed everything all legally, and moved to another town to give all three of us a new beginning away from gossiping tongues and any chance word that might leak out. After all, you can never tell when a peeping Tom might be listening at a keyhole. It wasn't easy, mind you. For a year, though she could speak, it was as though she was mute. That's why we didn't bring her to see you when you invited us. But by degrees we won her confidence, and she grew to be a docile, gentle and apparently normal child. Events before her real mother's death were never discussed. If she remembered anything she never said. But we rather imagined – Wilf and I – that the shock and maybe God's will, had sealed the horror off from her mind. Though sometimes I wondered–' Ellen's voice faltered vaguely.

'Yes?' Walter asked quietly. 'You wondered what, Ellen?'

'Well, she did have times when she wanted to be alone sometimes as I said. And she never seemed to laugh or want to have fun like other children. A vivid imagination, Wilf said it was, p'raps he was right. Anyway, when Wilf died I'd too much on my hands making a living for the two of us to brood on what Cassandra might be thinking about or fretting over in her 'alone' periods – that's what she called her solitary fits. It was always a relief to me when she came to you for holidays, because I knew Kate was a lively girl, and that she'd be well looked after, with a few of the comforts I couldn't give. Not that she wasn't fond of me, bless her, she was. But–' Ellen's voice suddenly grew tired, holding a hint of tears.

Emily got up and patted her shoulder. 'You just rest now, Ellen,' she said, 'try and relax. It's a sad story, and we both admire the way you carried on, and cared for that poor waif. Now we know everything it's easy for us to understand certain little slynesses in Cassie's nature. I blame myself for not having watched her more closely on that last day, but on the other hand you've said yourself she had "alone" times, and she seemed all right when she set off that day. I don't believe for a moment her death was anything but what the inquest said – accidental. It could just as well have happened in a town, that's what I tell myself when I think about it, she could've run under a bus, or been knocked down by a car. So we must try and cheer up and think about other things. I'll ring for a cup of tea now, for all three of us. Yes, Walter, you for once will have tea with us instead of your usual whisky.'

Walter grunted, had one look at his wife's face and did as he was told. Generally he held the reins, but when Emily grabbed them occasionally there was something forthright and determined about her that made others sit up and take notice.

7

When Rick suggested that Kate should accompany him to the Larchborough Annual Flower Show she was reluctant to go.

'The weather's so stuffy,' she said, 'and there'd be so much hanging about. And the petrol fumes upset me – as I am–' She gave an expressive little sigh. 'Please, Rick – you'll feel more free on your own.'

'For what?'

'Well, talking to people. Men friends.'

He gave a short laugh. 'You are funny, Kate. I can see my male friends when I like at any time. Another thing – Sir William, as chairman will expect us both, and I happen to be on the committee with a lovely wife to show off. As for petrol fumes, there won't be any. We'll have the carriage. Now don't argue, love, and don't pretend you're in such a delicate state you can't stand a few hours in the open air.' There was a pause and when she said nothing, he added, 'Can it be that you're a little shy of the Hon. Jon's discerning gaze upon you? If so, don't worry. You needn't be. Believe me, in that new frilly dress you've stung me for, no one will have the slightest suspicion of your budding condition.'

'Oh, don't be silly,' Kate snapped. 'What Jon thinks or doesn't think has nothing to do with it. He may not be there anyway.'

'He's sure to be,' Rick said. 'The whole family are determined to carry on with any official duties as normally as possible. Jon's taking a definite interest in his father's affairs since the tragedy; and the sooner the situation's accepted without embarrassment by his friends and relations the better for everyone concerned. Now don't sulk, darling. Determine to enjoy yourself, and you will. I want you with me.'

'And what *you* want you get; it's always the same,' she sighed.

'Not always, sweetheart. There've been countless occasions when you've cunningly contrived to get your own way without me having a clue at the time. So drop this senseless argument for Pete's sake. Come on now; smile.'

She didn't smile, but her face and body relaxed as he drew her to him and planted a gentle kiss on her cheek.

The weather remained fine for the flower show, and at eleven o'clock in the morning the field on the Wentworth estate, put aside annually as the site, was a blaze of colour with blooms of every variety and the summer dresses of feminine visitors.

Kate discovered that after all Rick had been correct in his estimate of her reaction once she was there. It was pleasant to be admired and a focus of male attention. Under her small lace-edged sunshade her face becomingly shadowed to a soft light, beamed entrancingly at Sir William's compliments although his wife's disapproval was obvious under the mask of a chill smile.

It was unfortunate that shortly before the time set for luncheon in the private tent reserved for VIPs that a rim of cloud emerged over the hills with the distant rumble of thunder.

There was movement in the crowd, and Rick, who was standing at a corner by the entrance, took Kate's arm, saying, 'May as well go in before the storm breaks.'

He pushed her ahead, and stopped short as a figure suddenly emerged from the opposite direction and only just avoided colliding with the Ferrises. Kate drew back sharply and gave a startled exclamation.

Jon.

Her heart quickened, not from pleasure, but from the impact of his expression, the cold look of fury – almost hate – on the bleak well-modelled features. Rick was about to speak, when Jon's voice cut through the air. 'How very opportune we should meet here. Haven't seen you for some time, Ferris. Or your wife.' He took a hasty glance round before resuming, 'And now, here we are, face to face, with no busybodies near to poke their noses into what should be quite a revealing little interview.' His mouth twisted. 'It will be short, I can assure you, and not very palatable – to you.'

Rick frowned and glanced at Kate: her face had whitened under the gauzy sun-shade.

'Well?' he demanded shortly, turning to Jon again, with his colour rising. 'Come on now, Wentworth. Out with it. If you've some little grudge about us better we should know and get the air cleared.'

'Exactly. Though I'd hardly call the matter of a human life "little".'

'Human *life*? What are you talking about?'

'Ask her. Ask the seductive Kate. *She* knows. Look at her. Ask *her* to explain. Or maybe I'd do it better – short and sharp – a man's way. Interested? Well, just picture the scene – you safely away in America, and Cass finding your devoted wife and myself making love in the Tree Studio. Oh, it had its charms in its own adulterous sexy way. But not to Cass. She'd been ill, remember? Nerves. And it killed her. *That's* what sent her to her death in that blasted pool. Get that into your mind once and for all, Ferris. It was Kate's spite and my own loneliness that killed the only woman I've ever wanted or truly loved–' He broke off, glassy-eyed with condemnation, hard lips set bitterly.

Rick's fist rose but Jon, quick as lightning, smartly avoided the threatened blow and, in a brief second, had disappeared into the tent. Kate clutched her husband's sleeve as he moved to follow. 'No. Don't – leave him,' she said, shocked by Wentworth's expression. 'It isn't true. He was lying – you *know* that, don't you? Rick, Rick, you must *believe* me. You must, you *must*. Don't you see? He's gone mad, because of Cass. And because – because–'

'Because what?'

'Oh, I don't know. I don't know. Only that–'

'Keep your voice down,' Rick interrupted. 'Obviously there's something I don't know about which should be discussed in private. I'll circulate the news you have a headache or the vapours, and regrettably have to return to Woodgate. So get out your smelling salts and put on a good show. Do you hear?' His grip tightened on her arm for an instant before releasing her and going to see about the carriage.

A few spots of rain fell as the carriage

made its way through the maze of wet lanes towards Woodgate, then the sky unpredictably lifted and the sound of thunder retreated eastwards. Kate made one attempt to ease the atmosphere by referring to Jon's 'wild mood', but Rick's cold response chilled her to silence for the rest of the way.

'This is not the time or place for discussing such matters,' he said, keeping his eyes firmly fixed on the back of Jed, their coachman's, back in its mustard-coloured coat and shining stove hat. 'Remember who you are.'

A furious retort was on Kate's lips, but she restrained any show of humiliation. In a way he was right, she thought, one shouldn't argue or divulge family differences before servants. All the same, her blood boiled, and her heart pumped wildly, not merely from anger but distress because Rick was so obviously going to be difficult and unnecessary over her unexpected meeting with Jon at the Tree Studio on that far off day when she'd tried to comfort him.

And she *had* tried, she told herself through a wave of self-pity. Of course perhaps she'd been unwise, under the circumstances. But Rick surely had sufficient faith in her to accept she'd felt nothing more than pity and friendship – a compassionate almost motherly wish to give help to another human being.

Or had he? Was his jealousy of her so abnormal it could warp things out of all proportion?

Doubt suddenly rose in her. He'd never really liked Jon. From their first meeting she knew he'd been secretly suspicious of her former romantic feeling for the Wentworth heir. But since then so much had happened. Everything had changed. She hadn't thought it possible that any shadow from the past could taint their own present passionate relationship.

It didn't occur to her to take the easiest and probably most successful course of denying there had been any meeting at all. There had been no interview. No one was aware of it but herself and Jon. If she stuck to that it would simply be her word against his, and Rick in the end would have to accept hers.

But Kate found it hard to lie. The truth to her was important especially in this case. Unless Rick accepted her explanation of the incident wiping out any doubts he had, their life together might never be the same again.

When at last they reached the house her whole body ached with tension. A housemaid entered the hall and Kate was about to offer an explanation when Rick, still wearing the set immobile expression, forestalled her. 'Your mistress is not feeling well,' he told the girl. 'See we are not disturbed.'

'Yes, sir. Is there anything I can get her?'

'No thank you, Annie,' Kate replied quickly, trying to conjure a smile to her dry lips. 'I found the heat trying.'

Rick kept his eyes steadily ahead, but the girl was not deceived.

'Something wrong between those two,' she said when she got back to the kitchen. 'The master and mistress. You should just have seen the look on his face! And she was all sort of trembling and hot and cold. My! I wouldn't like to be in *her* place, not for all the tea in China I wouldn't.'

At that same moment Kate was making a casual show of tidying her hair, and adjusting the frill of tulle at her neck. Rick had walked to the window overlooking the gardens and was standing with his hands behind his back, rigid except for an agitated movement of his fingers.

Suddenly he turned round and faced her. 'Well?' he said. 'When you've finished your unnecessary titivating perhaps we could start.'

She gave an almost imperceptible nervous jerk of her head. 'What? Oh, yes – of course. Jon.'

'Not only Jon, is it, Kate? According to him you played quite a part in that intimate little woodland scene.'

'Oh, but – it wasn't like he said,' she cried impulsively, going towards him. 'Really! Truly! There was nothing *between* us, Rick; he was in a dreadful state – about *Cass*. We hadn't *arranged* to meet there – not Jon and me. I expected *her*, but it was him. I had to talk to him, to try–'

'But you didn't only *talk*, did you?' His voice had hardened. *'Did* you?' Both hands enclosed on her forearms, his eyes held nothing but bitter condemnation.

She swallowed nervously. 'I – what do you suppose? I did just what any woman would. I tried to make him calm down, and that's the truth. Comfort him. He was hysterical, Rick–'

'And you consider it your destiny to go round comforting hysterical men while your husband was conveniently out of the way, or should I say just one man – your blond ex-lover?'

She flushed. 'That's a horrid thing to say, and very, very unfair.'

He let her go, took a deep breath and remarked, 'I'm afraid I don't believe you, and I'm a fool even to be discussing the matter with you. Jon had no reason to fabricate such an incident. And knowing what I know of you, my dear, the interlude wouldn't end with a mere kiss.' He paused, then continued, 'I should like to appear the compliant understanding husband, but the fact is I understand too well. You've always lusted after Wentworth, and took the first chance when I was off the map of grabbing what you could of him.' His temper was quickly rising. 'I've never struck a woman in my life, but at this moment, if it wasn't for your condition, I could gladly forget any shred of gentlemanly manners I possess and beat you – if it would help, but it wouldn't. When we married I knew how you felt about Wentworth, it must have been obvious to anyone who was interested, but I believed I could wipe him out of your heart with perseverance and time. Obviously I was wrong. So this is it. I've no use for a faithless wife. It's best we should both accept it with the minimum of fuss–'

'But Rick – Rick–'

He turned his back on her and went to the door. 'I shall be back later. There need be no scandal. We'll discuss plans when I can bear the sight of you again.'

The door closed.

He was gone.

The echo of his footsteps fading down the stairs was like a knell sounding in her head.

She flung herself on the bed face down and after a few moments the tears were wet on the pillow.

How could he be so mean and cruel? She wondered desperately clutching her handkerchief into a tight damp ball against her cheek. Not even to have listened to her, just taken Jon's accusation as the truth?

Jon had obviously been acting in revenge against her, to ease his own feelings concerning Cass.

Cassandra had been mentally sick for months – all the family knew that, but even if she'd put the very worst construction on what she'd seen, that fateful afternoon, it wouldn't have driven her to suicide – that's what Jon's wild outburst had implied.

Why? *Why*? Why? Pondering the pillow Kate told herself with a renewed burst of emotion that somehow she'd make Rick see sense and believe her. He was unbalanced at the moment, shocked beyond all reason by a calculated evil lie. But tonight perhaps he'd have things more in perspective.

He'd said he'd be back later to talk – make plans or something. Plans for what? An icy wave of fear shivered down her spine. Did he mean to leave her? But he wouldn't. There were the children and the one to come, and he had no legitimate cause for a separation. If he suggested it she'd throw that horrible Mrs Linda Wade in his face – publicize how they still met in London sometimes – she knew that was true, he hadn't denied it – and all the district would be on her side. Anyway, harming each other wouldn't help either, she decided miserably. Her only real weapon was herself – to make herself so beautiful and desirable he couldn't resist her and would believe intuitively in her innocence.

Her mind darted here and there. What time would he be back? And what would she wear? After a short period of pondering she swung herself out of bed, went to the wardrobe and pulled out a number of hangers displaying a variety of housecoats and negligées. Her tears had temporarily dried now, and she looked absurdly young with her hair loose and curling over her wet forehead. She held the first one up before her surveying her reflection through the mirror, then another, and another, followed by a fourth. She chose the last – pale lilac see-through chiffon that she'd worn on her honeymoon. It was very full, sufficiently so to disguise her developing waistline, yet still enhance the blossoming curves of her lovely body. A tentative little smile touched her lips. Everything would be all right, she told herself optimistically. She'd have a lovely scented bath in the meantime, using the favourite very expensive perfume he'd last given her. And when he came through the bedroom door she'd be waiting for the sweet and heady reconciliation which had always followed their slightest misunderstanding.

Only it didn't quite happen that way.

It was eight o'clock before Rick returned, and during the whole afternoon and evening Kate had eaten nothing but an apple, and nibbled a few biscuits. She had stayed upstairs, and refused lunch and dinner on the pretext of being unwell. Therefore when Ferris *did* appear, looking jaded and still grim, her nerves were taut beneath her glamorous exterior, and her practised 'innocent' smile of welcome didn't quite register in the way she'd intended.

He sniffed the air and waved a hand. 'Is this for my benefit?'

She flushed. 'It's the perfume we chose together. That expensive one. Oh, Rick–' She moved towards him tentatively, hands slightly raised. 'I've been so miserable.'

He looked resolutely away from the limpid pleading of her lovely eyes. '*Please* let us be friends.'

'For heaven's sake, Kate, I'm tired and in no mood for dramatics.' There was a pause. 'I've thought everything out, and in my mind it's settled.'

'What is? What's settled?'

'Our mutual existence, my dear. Our – cohabitation, if you like; only it won't exactly be that.'

'What do you mean?'

All colour left her face. She rushed forward and caught the lapels of his coat, gripping and pulling them until he managed to free himself. Then, adjusting his tie and rubbing a hand wearily over his forehead, he said, 'Sit down, Kate. Keep a little dignity whatever else you've lost.'

All energy suddenly drained from her. She perched rigidly on the side of the bed and asked again, 'What do you mean? *Lost*? I've a right to know.'

'A faithless wife has no right.'

In spite of her distress her temper rose. 'No. That's just it. Because you think or *want* to think that Jon and I had an affair in your absence, *I'm* in the wrong and the one to blame; just because I'm a woman. Because you're a man you can do anything you like and get away with it. It's not fair. But one day it will be different. You see! And what about the Wade woman–?' She broke off breathlessly.

'What about her?' His voice was icy.

She started to sob again. 'Oh, go away. Leave me alone.'

'I'll do that soon enough when I've told you what I've decided to do.'

The tears stopped. She stiffened and looked at him sharply, rigid-backed. '*You!* Always you.'

'Yes. As you say. This is my home, my estate, and the two children are also mine–'

'Ours.'

'Naturally, as their mother.'

'And of the one to come,' she couldn't help adding.

'And its father? What about its father?'

It was a moment before the intended insult sank in, then she said bitterly, 'How *could* you? Do you realize how perfectly beastly you're being?'

He shrugged. 'Yes. But it's true, isn't it? How do we know?'

'I see. *That's* what's been festering in your mind. That Jon and I – that–'

'It's quite a natural possibility – under the circumstances.' For the first time the coldness of his face changed to sadness. 'I didn't want things this way,' he told her more quietly. 'I loved you, Kate – I could still love you, as much – more perhaps – than any man ever loved – if this whole business could be wiped out. But after I left you this morning I went to see Jon intending to kick his guts out. Instead I listened. He was – different. He looked half dead. Gaunt. I couldn't half kill an ill man. But his story was the same. I believed him.'

'And so?' she managed to say.

'You and I will behave like civilized human beings,' he told her emotionlessly, 'to the outside world. But as individuals apart. No one need know the real state of affairs. You will appear socially as my wife, and act as hostess to any guests I have here. I shall be away a good deal, and frequently spend nights at my club. Luckily we already have the large adjoining dressing-room and bedroom. So there will be no sleeping problems.'

'I see.'

'I hope you do, and will act with propriety befitting your position. Not only for our mutual sakes, but for the children's – especially the little stranger on the way.'

He waited for her reaction, watching her shrewdly.

She lifted her head inches higher and remarked, 'So now you're threatening me over the child.'

'No. I'm *reminding* you of its position. In every practical way it will be treated as mine–'

'It *will* be yours,' she interrupted.

'But we don't know, do we?'

'Oh!' Suddenly all life seemed to drain out of her. She flung herself into an arm chair and lay back with her head on its silk cushion. Then surprisingly she heard him say in perfectly ordinary tones, 'You must be tired. Can I get you anything?'

She shook her head dumbly and closed her eyes. A moment later she heard his footsteps cross the floor to the door. He paused a moment and said, 'I'll be careful not to disturb you when I return. It may be late. I shall use the other key.' Then he was gone.

8

As high summer gradually turned to autumn the weather became grey and cloudy with morning and evening mists frequently thickening to thin fog. The new domestic routine at Woodgate took shape according to Rick's plan. Kate, who felt more tired during this pregnancy than when she'd had the twins, would not have objected to the separate sleeping arrangements for herself and Ferris under more agreeable circumstances – indeed sometimes she could have welcomed it but the cause of the sterile relationship between herself and her husband depressed her and increased her feeling of being deprived and unwanted. The household staff, although sensing a strain in the atmosphere were forced to accept the marital arrangement as probably correct and sensible. There was a certain obvious air of tension about their mistress – a lack of joy – that suggested she was over-tired.

'It's more than tiredness, if you ask me,' Cook confided to the housemaid. 'Either she's ill, or there's something wrong between them two. She doesn't seem to notice anything properly any more. Oh, I'm not saying she doesn't fuss about the house. More than she used to, I'll grant you that – the mistress never was one before to bother about a bit of dust, or having things in the right place. But now she's forever up and down – moving this here, that there, with a kind of fussed, tight look on her face as though she was fretting over something but couldn't make out what it was. And the children; mostly she doesn't seem to bother about them one bit, although–' there was a significant pause before the oration continued – 'the other day when I went into the garden to hurry Jake with the greens I passed her – the mistress – on the back drive – she'd been talking to the nursemaid who'd got the little one in that pram, and there were tears in her eyes. I wasn't mistaken – actually *tears*. What do you make of that?'

Annie, the housemaid, shrugged. 'Women go funny sometimes when they're expecting,' the girl commented. 'Moods. It's like eatin', they fancy funny things. My aunt Mary—'

'Oh, don't go through all that again. How your Aunt Mary had a passion for frogs' legs when she was in the family way just because she'd been on a holiday trip to France once where her cousin was training to be a chef. Enough of it, young Annie. This isn't the time for old tales and gossip. We've both got things to do.'

In this way speculation continued from time to time. Whisperings and conjectures went on in an undertone, but the social life of Woodgate was superficially normal. Kate entertained Rick's friends and business acquaintances whenever necessary with polite, if somewhat stony, competence and a veneer of dignity betraying no suspicion of anything disruptive in the household. But beneath her cold armour, there was a wild and restless anger at the unfairness, and Jon's treachery.

One day in early September when Rick

was away for the week in London, she made a point of driving herself in the dog-cart to a spot bordering Charnbrook at a time she knew Jon generally passed by during his round of the estate. She was lucky in her reckoning. She was turning a corner of a lane edging a field, when he appeared, luckily on foot. He was presumably on his way to a nearby small tenant farm.

He gave her a brief sidelong glance and would have passed on, but she reined and stopped the cart with a jerk, calling, 'I want a word with you, Jon.' Her heart was pounding; from the shrill note in her voice he knew she intended a confrontation.

He stepped aside. 'Certainly. Can I assist you down, Mrs Ferris.'

She flushed, knowing the remark held an inference to her size.

'No. You know what I want,' she said, when she'd extricated herself from the dog-cart. 'The truth.'

His eyes narrowed. They held an expression she couldn't fathom – triumph, or was it a kind of suppressed wary rage. Certainly there was no pity or warmth.

'About what?'

In spite of her determination to appear calm even conciliatory, in the hope he'd co-operate and somehow admit the truth to Rick, or in writing, her blood boiled with renewed indignity.

'Don't pretend,' she said, as the rosy colour deepened in her cheeks. 'That lie – that dreadful thing you told Rick about – about the day Cass found us in the Tree Studio when he was in America – that we'd been making love. You *know* it isn't true. Then *why?* Oh, Jon.' Her voice softened. '*Please* put it right. I know you were upset about – about losing Cass – that was why I was trying to–'

'Seduce me?' His voice cut the air like a knife.

Her mouth opened. 'How *dare* you?' she gasped.

Jon gave a short laugh of derision. 'Oh, stop the dramatics, Kate. Don't try the innocent on me. You *wanted* me then. You always have, haven't you? From the very first chance you had of fluttering your eyes at me. Do you imagine others didn't know it? Your parents? Ferris himself? And when the chance came of getting me alone at the Tree Studio you jumped at it. You'd been watching that day, hadn't you? Because you'd somehow found out Cass wasn't going to be there and you'd have me alone, but she changed her mind. I was in a state, I admit. But not too far gone not to know what you were up to. Oh, yes! You have very soft lips, Kate, *hungry* lips. It was *sex*, Kate, wasn't it? *Sex*. And Cass!' For a moment his face slackened and quivered. 'She *knew*, she *saw*. And it *killed* her. So don't talk about love, and comfort, because you don't know the first thing about either.'

'You have a foul rotten mind,' Kate cried, suddenly throwing any sense of discretion to the winds. 'If Rick was here, he'd–'

'He'd what? Presumably he thinks as I do. Too bad. For you. But don't imagine I'll lift a finger to put things right for you. You *killed* Cass, and may accept the consequences. I'll never forgive you. *Never.*'

She half-lifted her whip to strike him, then let her arm drop, shocked by the renewed blaze of hatred on his face, and the realization that he really meant it. He really believed she was responsible for her cousin's death and was wanting revenge for that dreadful day.

Numbly she watched him turn and stride away, cutting down a narrow path between high hedges to the little farm. Hopelessness engulfed her. She could see no way now of persuading Rick to accept the truth. Jon was obviously beyond reason over the matter of Cass, and there was no one else to help her.

She didn't know how she was going to bear life without her husband's love.

Even the thought of the coming child was a torment and she wished at this juncture it had never been conceived.

When Rick returned from London he informed her that some wealthy Americans had arrived at Charnbrook on his instructions, with the intention of looking over the Dower House, being interested in purchasing the property for holiday and business.

'We shall be expected at the Wentworths' for dinner the following Monday,' he said with a quick probing glance at his wife, 'and

I hope you'll put on as good a show of conviviality as possible. The name of the American is Carcodale. Hiram Carcodale. He's already an important personality in the USA moving-picture project, and is anxious to make the acquaintance of certain theatrical personalities over here for our mutually planned magazine. They're a Boston family with one daughter, I believe, and contact with the Wentworths, an example of the English aristocracy, will mean a good deal to them.'

Kate's temper exploded.

'You mean after what happened – after the scene with Jon and – and allowing him to get away with such rotten lies, you expect *me* to go to Charnbrook as a guest and pretend to be a friend of theirs – well!' She turned and faced him fiercely, with a rustle of skirts – they were standing in the conservatory. 'I won't do it. It's asking too much. Go if you must – if your – your loyalty to the Wentworths and your American moving-picture friends is stronger for them than for your wife. But of course' – her lip curled, though the threat of tears choked in her throat – 'it obviously does, or we shouldn't be leading this sterile life–' She broke off breathlessly staring.

'If you've quite finished,' he said, 'we can perhaps talk sanely for a change?' His face was as expressionless as a block of wood, although behind the façade his emotions churned with a wild desire to treat her as one might treat a rebellious child, followed by the pleasure of making-up, of sweeping the bundle of sweet sensuality into his arms in a flood of desire. She was wearing green, shining leaf-green that, against her cream skin and gleaming dark hair, imbued her with the quality of some rare exotic flower. He wanted her. Following the first week of their rift he'd never been free of a repressed need and longing for her supine satin-smooth limbs entwined with his – for the feel of his lips pressed against her skin, during the intimacy of deepest human experiences, of man's love for woman. But forgiveness evaded him. Love, he decided, the gentle sentimental love expressed romantically in novels through the ages, was seemingly not in his nature. He had been soured beyond endurance by his conviction that another man had trespassed on his most private and precious of preserves. She was tainted – no longer the perfect pearl of his existence. But she still belonged; and whenever necessary he meant to see she recognized it.

When she remained silent he said with an effort, 'I hope you understand. There must be no sign of disruption between us.'

'I said I would not go.'

'But you will, won't you? You're not ill; you'll probably enjoy meeting the Carcodales. And' – his glance became a little kinder – 'for your benefit it's hardly likely you'll see much of Jon. He'll be otherwise engrossed, discussing a certain business matter with Hiram that will take him back with them to the USA. I shall be thankful myself to be rid of the sight of him, and I've a shrewd idea the Wentworths will jump at the idea. It concerns photography – quite Jon's line. I've already a new bailiff lined up part-time for Sir William and his lady wife's worries over their neurotic son will be put at rest. So, for God's sake, Kate, take that look off your face and make the best of things–'

'If you had a shred of love for me left, you–'

'*If* is a very useful word,' he interrupted, 'but hardly at this point,' and he turned away without another glance at her.

9

On Sunday afternoon, before the arranged dinner party at Charnbrook, Emily and Walter visited Woodgate to make sure everything was well with their daughter and family, and with the information that they also had been invited to meet the American guests the following evening.

Rick had a wary look in his eyes for Kate as his in-laws gave the news. During the week his wife had been stubbornly silent about the subject whenever he referred to it and, although he had little doubt she'd agree to going without a further scene, still with Kate he could never be a hundred per cent certain. So he was relieved when she merely said with cool, apparent indifference, 'Oh, yes, I shall be there, although I expect it will be rather boring. But Rick doesn't fancy appearing without me. I suppose in America it would be considered infra-dig for one to go without the other. Aren't they very family-minded in Boston?'

A slight frown puckered Emily's forehead. 'I don't know about that.' After a slight pause she continued, 'You feel all right, don't you, dear? You're not overtired or anything?'

Kate sighed. 'Don't fuss, Mama. Why should I be tired? What have I to do?'

'Well, with a house to run, two young children to care for, and another on the way, I should have thought there was plenty,' Emily retorted a little more sharply.

'Nursemaids and servants have their duties and they don't like being interfered with,' Kate answered shortly. 'And Rick's fussy over me not lifting anything or attempting any household chores in my – delicate state, although I must say he expects a good deal of me as a hostess.'

Emily was troubled.

As they drove away she said to Walter, 'I'm concerned about our girl; she seems bitter over something, and that's not like Kate.'

'Forget it,' Walter remarked, although he was bothered himself. 'You can't do any good by fretting. Families have good days and bad days. If there was anything really troubling her she'd let us know. As far as I can see Ferris makes a good husband, and they're fond of each other.'

'They *were*.'

'What do you mean – *were*?'

'Before all this moving-picture business got such a hold on him. A woman wants other things than business about her when she's expecting. But whenever we've seen him lately – not often I grant you – still, each time he's on about America and future this, future that – so you hardly know where you are. There's other things than money too. Were you any happier after you made your pile, Walter? No. Life's easier, of course, we see places, and have things we'd not got before, but it's only the kind of *way* we lived that's different not the quality. You've always had a thought for me. But Rick these days seems forever bent on going somewhere else and grabbing something new. A real buccaneer!'

Walter laughed. 'Come on now, Emily, you're imagining things.'

Buccaneer, he thought, the very idea. And yet in a way apt. Ferris did have a certain dominant 'eagle' look about him these days.

He did his best to dispel the slight discomfort Emily's words had caused him, and on the appointed evening the American couple arrived at Charnbrook looking the picture of well-contented, middle-class affluence. To Rick's satisfaction the men found instant rapport, possessing a similar down-to-earth recognition of a changing new world ahead. Both though sturdy patriots to their own soil, had a hankering to have a 'finger in the other's pie' – a nibble of a social and business crust, so to speak.

Hiram to look at was large, slightly portly, with a genial smile and shrewd dark eyes that suggested a hint of Mexican forebears, rather than the Scots ancestry he boasted of. Eileen, his wife, referred to her connection to a Cornish grandfather who had emigrated to America during the mining crisis. She was small and plump, displaying diamonds that must have cost a fortune and a vital personality and laugh that inevitably reduced any faint unease of shyness in the party to a minimum. Only Olivia, despite a façade of graciousness, remained subtly aloof. She was watching Jon from time to time. He made it his business to avoid Kate as much as possible, which wasn't difficult as Kate kept in the vicinity of her mother and Hiram's wife. At dinner she was placed between her mother and the American's daughter.

Elizabeth Carcodale, a rather gaunt, tall, horsy-looking girl, obviously found Jon attractive. She was not good-looking, but neither was she plain, and she certainly had the gift of conversation and telling an amusing tale. In spite of himself, Jon found he hadn't lost the ability to smile. After dinner, while Wentworth took Rick and the older men to the billiard-room for a smoke and Olivia entertained the feminine guests in the drawing-room, Jon was diverted from any chance embarrassing encounter with Kate by a request from Elizabeth to show a collection of his photography – mostly stables of horses – a wish encouraged enthusiastically by her mother, and approved by Olivia, only grudgingly, since it meant a private session for the two young people in the Hon. Jon's study, which was not, on such a short acquaintance, exactly protocol. Still, in this case, considering her son's distressed state of mind, and the fact that he would probably be leaving with the Americans when they returned to the States, such a point as convention appeared almost a triviality. Anything was better than seeing him as he was; and as William had pointed out earlier, a possible friendship between the two young people could ease many of their financial problems. It was unfortunate from a traditional point of view that money nowadays seemed to be in so many wrong hands, socially. In Olivia's young days a girl with such a dreadful accent would never have been accepted by the aristocracy. But if anything *did* come out of this new acquaintanceship – and she sensed William himself had given the idea an optimistic thought – he really seemed to have no sense of true pride these days – the couple would not be under their feet all the time, but mostly those long miles away across the Atlantic in Boston.

The result of that evening was more amicable than might have been expected from Kate's point of view. Rick agreed to leave Charnbrook at an early hour which meant the removal of any undercurrent of stress in the gathering, leaving Jon free to discuss Hiram's proposal for him as publicity trainee and photographer with the new moving-picture firm in America.

The Carcodales decided to leave Britain earlier than was expected, after acquiring the Dower House at a considerably higher price than had been expected by the Wentworths.

During the few weeks before departure Jon's nerves relaxed and, fortified by his deepening friendship for Elizabeth Carcodale he was able to look back on the past tragedy of Cass's death more reasoningly. He realized the cruelty of his own behaviour to Kate, but considered she'd deserved it, recalling the compulsive heady sexuality of her presence and her closeness to him on that dreadful day. She should never have been there, he told himself more than once, as the memory swept over him.

However much she might deny it – she'd *wanted* him. Secret lusting was as bad as technical unfaithfulness; and in retrospect he decided anything could have happened in those heady moments of anguish, loss and longing.

Thus he forced himself to reason in justification over his damning confrontation with Rick. It was right he knew the type of woman he'd married. And anyway Ferris was no saint himself. So let them solve their own future, which no doubt would be what they deserved.

America lay ahead.

Once there, in a new enterprising and remunerative occupation he might, in time, be able to erase the torture of Cass's death to the back of his mind – even eventually to forgetfulness.

In this way Jon's problem was solved.

10

Kate expected her baby in December, and by November there were times when she wondered how she'd ever get through to the date. Rick was away a good deal and, although during the times he was at Woodgate he was polite and always saw she had everything for her comfort, he remained aloof and succeeded in an unsmiling way of shutting her from his personal life.

She went to bed early those days; if both happened to be in a lounge or the drawing-room, he would be quick to open the door for her, incline his head and say a brief 'Goodnight', but there was never a touch between them – no contact at all unless it was a brief brush of silk as she passed, followed by the closing of the latch, and her figure moving into the shadows by the stairs.

Every night he was at Woodgate she would lie wakeful, sometimes for hours, listening with ears keyed and senses alert in the wild hope of his footsteps emerging along the landing, and not pausing until he came to her own door. Then the pause and turn of the knob, and he would be there at last in his rightful place, a tall figure looking down on her – Rick! her husband and lover.

But it never happened.

At first, during the long estrangement she'd told herself it would be different when the baby came. He would *know* it was his. He'd *have* to – she'd somehow prove it. And if it was a boy – but now even that eventuality failed to rouse her. She was too exhausted to hope any more.

'You look tired,' Rick said surprisingly one day. 'Do you see the doctor regularly?'

A flicker of life stirred in her. 'He calls every day. But of course you wouldn't know being in London so much. He says I'm all right.'

'Good. It would be a pity for the twins to have an ailing mother so young in life.'

The brief warmth in her froze. The twins!

Marged and Felicity! – always the twins. It was as though he cared for nothing of his own but his possessions, his business and the two tiny girls he knew were his. At first in the early period of the rift she'd been jealous of the sudden look of ardour on his face whenever he looked on them, the blaze of tenderness in his dark eyes. Now she felt merely dull resentment; she wished frequently she had no children at all. During his brief periods at Woodgate he made it so increasingly clear that she personally was merely a chattel in his life.

In early November she decided she couldn't stand it any longer. Rick was away on a brief visit to London, and would be returning that night. She had been sleeping badly recently, partly due to the restlessness of the baby that should be born in a few weeks, but mostly the result of her deep unhappiness. Why should it be so? Why should she be forced into such a hell of misery at such a time and for something that was no fault of her own? Well, perhaps she'd been a little unwise with Jon that fateful day, she thought at times. But there were better, kinder things than wisdom. Rick was wise in a shrewd cold way – in business, in stocks and shares and companies and getting his own way. And 'having and holding'. But love? His love had proved sterile. And she so needed love at this time – *someone's* – if not his. Suddenly she knew. She wanted her mother, and her father's whimsical way of cracking a joke, as he had done when she was upset over anything when she was a little girl. Yes, it was her parents she wanted, with their arms round her so she could cry and cry, and let her grief explode, freed by the comfort of their presence.

She would go to them.

She would go that day before Rick got back, and stay. Her child should be born at Beechlands. Somehow she'd think of an excuse – that Rick was too much away, and she wasn't well, or – oh, something. *Something.* They would understand. They always had. There'd be no need for details. Just one thing was clear. She had to get to them.

The nursery staff were engaged with the children upstairs and the rest of the domestics busy about the kitchen when Kate set off shortly before twelve that morning for Beechlands.

She was wearing a long, thick, grey, hooded cape, and carried only a very light case. No one had a glimpse of her except a gardener from the potting shed, as she cut down a side lane to the paddock. From there she planned to take a short cut along a path through a patch of forest land which led into the lane eventually going to the main road. It would be possible to catch a country bus at the crossroads, she thought vaguely. If not, there would surely be someone willing to give her a lift, a farmer, or friend possibly.

It was very cold. Her mind was exhausted and confused, and her body felt unduly heavy that day. She'd have to think up some explanation she supposed – an excuse for being out on her own wandering in her condition. But just then practical things didn't seem to matter. She was driven by one compelling thought – to get home.

Hazily she recalled the note she'd written to Rick before leaving Woodgate:

Rick, don't come looking for me. I'm leaving you, and I'm not coming back. Our life lately has been a mockery. There's no need to worry about me. Where I'm going I shall be perfectly all right. And you have the twins.
    Goodbye.
                                        Kate.

It was strange how clearly the words remained in her mind. As she plunged into the spreading thicket of trees through the gate the bare dark branches of trees jigged like immense letters before her eyes in the rising wind – '*I'm never coming back – never coming back.*' From the leaden sky above flakes of snow fell in only a thin flurry at first, then thicker, filming branches and ground below with white.

She blinked and drew her cloak closer, lifting a cold hand to wipe the frost from her eyes. Soon, as the woodland enclosed the world outside, the path thinned, disappearing at points, emerging only fitfully in treacherous snake-like twists and turns. Her senses became numbed and disorientated; gradually she was aware of nothing any more but the increasing heaviness of her own body, the urgency for sanctuary and rest. But no rest came, only a crippling stab of pain that sent her reeling for support to the trunk of a birch. She clung there till the first agony passed, then went on again. How long she'd been continuing haphazardly between bouts of giddiness and pain, clutching her distended stomach, searching desperately for guidance she had no idea. But at last, like a miracle, a faint rosy glow emerged from a small clearing behind a clump of thorns – only a flicker at first, but a sign of life surely, she thought, suddenly wildly alert – indication of a lamp? Or glow from a fire? A window perhaps? That of a cottage near the road?

With a spurt of energy she made an effort to break through the tangled undergrowth, but it was too much for her. Brambles clawed her face as she fell. Renewed agony struck her with the sensation of a sword splitting her in two. Nothing registered any more but darkness and pain, and a terrible pushing, then a gigantic rush of relief followed by the thin high crying like that of a wild bird through the snow.

For a brief pause all was still in the forest, as though the thickening snow had laid its silent mantle over the earth. Even the wind was hushed. Then there was a crackle of branches and twigs, and the bent figure of the old Mumper emerged dark among the other shadows against the whitened earth. A transitory beam of crimson from his fire lit his bearded face, as he bent down where Kate lay with the newly-born child who was already hungry for the milk at her breast. Blood stained the ground; her eyes were shut. Awed, with a primitive fear gnawing his nerves he touched a cheek. The dark lashes parted and fluttered. Very slowly her tired gaze rested on the tiny wet head beside her. The man's withered countenance under the woollen cap jerked and nodded.

'It's all right, lady, I'll get 'elp. Where you b'long lady, eh? You tell old Mumper. That's me. I wont 'arm you, lady – not you nor that little 'un.'

But Kate was too exhausted to speak. Her eyes closed again and he hobbled off quickly through the undergrowth, anxious only to be away from a scene which might involve him with difficult questioning. It was an hour later before Kate was discovered by a search party organized by Rick who'd arrived back at Woodgate earlier than expected. The snow had thickened by then, and left no footsteps to guide them. The only clue they had was from a worker at a distant farm who'd glimpsed Kate's grey figure as she passed some distance away in the trees. Luckily for her he'd thought it strange, recognized her, and told the farmer who'd reported it to the house. This prompt action it was that saved her life and that of the baby who was later to be named Blanche-Rose.

11

The days passed into weeks and Kate lay for most of the time half-conscious in bed at Woodgate, after a bad attack of pneumonia followed by exhaustion. No one – not even her parents – was allowed to see her except Rick, and on the rare occasions of consciousness she turned her head away refusing to look at him. He spent much of each day in the room waiting for a sign of recognition, stony-faced and silent. But none came, no sign of emotion from the white face on the bed that could have been some marble effigy except for the luxurious surround of shadowed hair. She ate and drank what was held to her lips obediently, but without life or interest. With Blanche-Rose she would have nothing to do at all. Whenever her tiny prematurely-born daughter was brought to her, her eyes widened with something between terror and dislike; she'd put her head under the bedclothes and a muffled 'No – no' would come from her lips. No one had any idea why, except perhaps Rick who naturally kept the grim knowledge to himself.

The baby, with perfect tiny features, had a crop of very fine pale hair giving her at first glance an uncanny likeness to a miniature Jon.

Whatever feelings Rick might have had on the infant's perfect small features and extraordinary fair skin and pale hair, he made no comment except to say to the housekeeper, 'Another girl to name. Now what do you suggest, Mrs Rook?' Thinking it was a matter for Rick and Kate, but guessing he might already have asked and been rebuffed, Mrs Rook answered, 'Well now, what about Blanche? Isn't that French for "white"? And as she was born in the snow it seems fitting somehow.'

'Hm, and very cold,' he agreed with an underlying sting in his voice. 'Blanche? Yes, but let's have a bit of colour too. Rose, perhaps. Blanche-Rose. What do you think?'

'Oh, Mr Ferris, sir, that's perfect. And

suitable too with that pink little bud of a mouth.'

So the matter was settled as quickly as that.

Comment was naturally caused in the kitchen when the name was known, and Cook was critical of Mrs Rook. 'Pretty enough,' she said, 'but a bit fancy. To my mind the mistress might have shown an interest. It's not right the master should have to shoulder such things on his own. And if what I heard's true the doctor says there's nothing wrong with Madam now except exhaustion following the pneumonia and that night in the snow. If you ask me, things are sometimes made too easy for rich folk–'

'But no one *has* asked you,' came the tart reply. 'Mr Ferris has the right. It's his choice, and no one else's to criticize.'

During the first fortnight of Kate's recovery following the crisis of her illness Emily and Walter had been allowed to see their daughter and the baby for a few minutes; but it was not a success.

Although so weak, Kate was by then aware

of the gossip that must have emerged over her flight from Woodgate, and was resentful of wagging tongues that might have upset them. This happened to be true. The note, for instance, had been seen by a maid on the dressing-table before Rick returned, and the envelope was not stuck down. She could have opened it, probably had, the girl was only human, and had a boyfriend. It was hardly likely she hadn't dropped a hint to him; then the old Mumper, having been treated to a pint at a wayside inn after his wanderings that evening, had told a garbled tale about a fine lady wandering all bloodied in the woods. There was the farmworker – a word here, a word there – their strange stories that couldn't be disproved.

For a time the Ferris family was bound to be a source of wild conjecture and rumours.

So when Emily tried with soothing words to get at the truth, at the same time doing her best to comfort her daughter, Kate passed a hand over her forehead and said, 'Oh, do leave me alone Mama. So many questions, and I'm so tired. I don't want your sympathy. *Please*.'

Her quick flashing glance at her mother was so intense Emily was hurt. And, with a hint of annoyance said, 'Very well. If that's how you feel to those who care for you, I'm sure your father and I don't want to intrude.' She picked up her handbag and went to the door. Walter followed, looked back with a placating gesture to the bed, shook his head, winked and raised a finger to his lips.

'Shsh,' he murmured, and blew a kiss before disappearing after Emily.

Following this unsatisfactory interlude it was some time before Emily visited Woodgate again, and by then Kate was mobile and able, the doctor said, to get dressed and go downstairs when she felt like it. But her lethargy continued, and she still took no apparent interest in tiny Blanche-Rose whose fragile looks and fairness dis-turbed her, bringing always a bitter reminder of Jon. That she could bear a child so unlike herself or Rick was ironic. She was under no illusion that her husband had not noticed it. But he said nothing. He remained polite, thoughtful, though outwardly cold.

Once he said on his morning visit to enquire about her health, 'I hope you approve of my choice of name for the baby?'

She was standing by the french window, wearing a sea-green velvet housecoat with her rich hair loose on her shoulders. She turned and answered with chill indifference, 'I don't care what she's called.'

'Then I think perhaps you should,' he told her. 'In the doctor's opinion it would be better for you now if you could bring yourself to take a little interest in the normal things of life.'

She regarded him coolly and replied with no sign of emotion on her face, 'But things aren't normal here, are they?'

His mouth half-opened to speak, then he thought better of it, and closed it, turned away and made to leave.

'I hope you have a good day,' he said a moment later. 'I'm going to London and won't see you again until tomorrow. So if you're wise you'll make your mother welcome if she decides to call. And try and look a little more cheerful. Harshness doesn't suit you.'

The latch clicked; she was alone.

He was not to know how, after a moment or two, her tension broke, and she flung herself on the bed with tears gushing from her eyes. Nor had she any idea of the futility he felt – the sense of failure, and sterility of an existence without the woman to whom at that moment he would gladly have sacrificed all else he possessed if she'd wanted it.

Later he was ashamed of his own fleeting emotional lapse, and stayed in London an extra day. During that time he had dinner with Linda Wade, but if she had any optimistic hopes the occasion was meant to convey a feeling on his part of more than mere friendship, she was disappointed. She quickly discovered – despite the excellent champagne they drank – that his thoughts were elsewhere, and correctly divined where. That something was wrong between him and his young wife became painfully obvious – not through what he said, but what he did not; and later after bidding her a cordial but abstracted, 'Good night,

Linda,' adding, 'It's been nice seeing you again,' she gave a regretful smile and rueful shake of the head.

'But not nice enough,' she said. 'I never was, was I? Never mind, we've the magazine and business in common. But your heart's with Kate, and I reckon it always will be. So get back on the next train, that's my advice; a good thing's worth hanging on to.'

He did just that, and arrived at Lynchester in the early hours of the morning.

It was 4 a.m. when Rick inserted his key into his own front door and entered the house. He walked as quietly as possible along the wide hall and up the main staircase to the first floor and his study. Having dozed on and off through the journey from London he was not so physically tired as mentally. Instead of providing the emotional ballast he'd hoped for from his interlude with Linda, the meeting had proved to be merely dead sea fruit – a proof of a lack in his life that could be filled completely by only one woman – Kate.

For the first time in his life he was faced

with a problem he felt unable to solve. His mind – usually so needle sharp and clear was torn ruthlessly in two directions – one the unquenchable desire for her and to believe in her innocence concerning Jon Wentworth, the other to follow the line of reasoning and common sense, taking her story with a grain of salt, but outwardly accepting it because he needed her so much. The latter course perhaps might eventually end in complete forgiveness. On the other hand the shadow could always linger between them.

Who could say?

Wearily, feeling curiously drained and defeated, he entered his study and lit the incandescent wall lamp. It was still dark outside, although the pale thin grey of dawn would soon be lifting over the gardens spreading a blurred light against the Gothic-styled long widow. At the moment everything in the book-lined interior was a cheerless pattern of shadowed distorted forms – cupboards and office equipment, plus the addition of a large leather armchair and sofa and valuable antique secretaire.

A man's room.

No lingering aroma of feminine perfume here, no glimmer of a woman's white arms and shadowed sweet smile.

No Kate.

Just chill negation of emotion. A reminder of finance and committee, sterile business days ahead. He flung his scarf over the table, fetched a decanter and glass from the cabinet and poured a stiff drink, taking it neat. Then he slumped into the armchair, stretched out his legs and threw his head back against the leather cushion. Gradually the liquor warmed his spirits. But, despite the fact he was still wearing his coat, the early morning spring air felt chill. He braced himself to move, not worth lighting the fire. Soon there'd be the first sounds of domestic life beginning from the kitchen below. He reached for his scarf and went upstairs to the quarters he now occupied. In spite of his efforts to make no noise, the door creaked when he unlocked it and went in.

Then the shock hit him.

The small round lamp glowed by the bed, and someone was lying there. A woman. He stood quite still for a moment angered by this violation of his privacy until, as he stepped forward, he saw who it was, the first reaction collapsed, shattered by bewilderment that was almost disbelief.

Kate.

He approached the bed quietly. She was lying on her side with one cheek pressed against the pillow, her shining hair spread over the fine linen. The quilt was loose over her shoulders revealing the gentle curve of a breast under her blue silk nightdress. He bent down and saw she was sleeping, but he fancied the glint of tears still lingered on the soft thick fringe of her lashes; and there was something else – or was he mistaken? No. As he peered closer he recognized the collar of one of his own shirts protruding from the sheets. She was clutching it to her body as though it was a child or something she could not bear to be without.

Good heavens, he thought, completely disorientated by a conflict of emotions, had it been as bad for her as that?

His heart quickened. She appeared so young and vulnerable, only a girl in innocent dreamless slumber. Yet she was his wife and had already borne his children. That, and what else?

If only he knew. If only he could whisper her name, press his lips to hers gently, and watch those deep golden-dark eyes open with the truth clarified in their clear gaze.

But he had not the heart or the will to wake her at that moment for fear of what he found there. As he waited she stirred. He turned away, and swiftly, quiet-footed as a panther, crossed the thick carpet in three strides and was closing the door behind him.

No doubt she'd soon be fully awake and back in her own bedroom. She'd better be, he thought, with a touch of wry humour, or heaven only knew what the maid would think who brought her early cup of tea, to find her mistress clutching a shirt in the master's room. Not that domestic gossip worried him any more. There'd been sufficient, as he well knew, to fill a book, concerning life at Woodgate during recent months. And none of it important or holding a grain of the tragic truth.

Which was? Again the same question.

He returned to his study, and knew suddenly that there had to be an answer. He and Kate had to face each other and solve the future. Life could not continue as it had.

In a flash an idea took shape from the conflict of his thoughts.

He went to his desk, took up pen and paper and wrote a short note.

Kate,

We have to talk.

I returned on the night train and am having an early breakfast before taking off to the stud.

Could we meet about 12 at Brad Hill? After long business sessions I need a leg stretch, and a dose of fresh air will do you good. You know the spot near the ancient Folly? – far enough away from Woodgate hopefully to get an objective clear slant on our relationship, but not too far to tire you.

I shall be waiting. If you don't make it, the meeting will have to be at the house, but I prefer otherwise.

Rick.

He stuck it down firmly, addressed it simply as KATE in his bold handwriting, and took it along the landing to a small semi-circular glass table standing against the wall immediately next to the door of their main bedroom. He left it there knowing she would see it when she left the room later for breakfast.

A sense of relief filled him. Whatever the outcome, at least some positive action must accrue. In his heart he knew he wanted and would have Kate, at any price – provided she told the truth without the sly ambiguities and protests of just wanting to comfort Wentworth. He was about to walk away when some quirk of fate made him put his hand unconsciously into a side pocket of his coat. There was a spare key there and a few loose coins. Something else too. Something soft. He drew it out.

A white velvet glove; crumpled now, but still seeming to hold a faint suggestion of perfume.

The shock of memory temporarily caught him off guard. All the time it must have lain there since the night of the dance those many years ago, simply because he'd worn that particular coat so rarely, and not being a sentimentalist he'd found no occasion or use for it.

Until now.

He placed it beside the note on the table for no logical reason whatever except perhaps to remind Kate of certain personal obligations, and a necessity at all costs for absolute truth between them as man and wife.

Then, hearing the subdued sound of movement from the bedroom he quickly made his way back along the corridor and down the stairs.

He decided to change clothes at the house by the stud, where his breeder kept certain accommodation for him, and have breakfast there. It was still sufficiently early for avoidance of a chance encounter with any servant of Woodgate, but the light outside was visibly lifting. So he made his exit as quickly as possible from a side door and five minutes later was well on his way.

12

An early haze had left the hills of Burnwood glittering bright with dew from the rising sun as Rick reached the high point of the Folly for his meeting with Kate.

He'd climbed the steep way leading from the historical parkland of Bradgate, but guessed Kate would naturally take the gentle field slope from the opposite direction. He had also expected her to be late – it was supposed to be a woman's prerogative – though he couldn't fathom why – in addition to which there was a stubborn streak in her to be reckoned with, and punctuality had never been one of her virtues.

He'd wandered restlessly about for over a quarter of an hour before he glimpsed her figure outlined against the shimmering sky. She was wearing a green cape and, as she approached, a rising breeze caught it up gently, revealing fleetingly the strong yet slender lines of her figure in its purple dress. She walked with a proud swing, chin up, nerves keyed no doubt to face him; a frail scarf tied loosely over her curls blew back behind her, taking flying strands of escaped russet hair with it.

He went to meet her, and they faced each other for a few moments not speaking. He thought she looked paler than usual, a little defiant. But beautiful. The epitome of some lovely legendary character made flesh and blood to taunt him. He gritted his teeth, forcing himself not to smile or take her as his instinct prompted into his arms.

'Well,' he said glancing down at his watch, 'so you've made it. I was beginning to wonder.'

'Naturally,' she answered. 'You ordered me.' Her tones were cool, impersonal.

He forced a short humourless laugh. 'Come, Kate, there's no need to fence with words. The time has come to settle things. For good. I don't intend to wear a hair shirt for ever, and I presume you want more from life than that of existence as an external grass widow.'

He noticed that the hard line of her lips relaxed slightly. She shrugged.

'What is it you're trying to say Rick? There's been so much discussion already. You've heard my explanation about – about Jon and everything so many times, and I just don't understand why we have to come here for more.'

'Don't you? It's one of my favourite places – rich with history – tragedy, comedy, yet still free for more. Happiness I hope. Come–' He touched her shoulder lightly, and strode to the sheltering walls of the ancient Folly which stood looking like a miniature castle on the highest point of the hill. The fresh green young bracken already sprinkled the rocky slope down to the valley below where a narrow river coursed over tumbled boulders catching silvered light from the sun. Deer were visible on the opposite side of the park moving gracefully through patches of woodland. Oaks thrived and the rich earth, though boggy in places immediately below the Folly, was riddled with rabbit holes.

A twisted thorn with dark gnarled arms

stood near a ruined mansion to the right, resembling some ancient witch for ever on the watch for trespassers. Kate had never particularly liked the spot, and said so. 'I prefer the Beacon,' she said. 'This is somehow sad.'

'Yes. It has atmosphere. I'm no romantic, as you know – not in words. But I believe we can learn through nature. Despite the freedom and beauty of this area now I always feel something of its past still lingers in the elements – of how that innocent young girl, Queen Jane for nine days, who lived at the ruined Hall, was manipulated and accused falsely by devious plotters and beheaded. But *you* know all about that. History books tell the story now, or half of it. But the truth of her suffering can never be recounted. That's what's so important – to know the truth. And *that* is all I ask of you, Kate.' There was a pause. 'Look at me.'

Very slowly she turned her head and stared straight into his face.

His gaze was relentlessly on hers. 'The *truth*,' he persisted, 'about you and Jon.'

She didn't answer, but turned with a

violent movement like that of some outraged wild thing and fled, cape flying, towards the stretch of lane she'd come along.

He caught up with her almost immediately and held her, struggling against him; it was then that self-control deserted him. His lips were on her mouth, cheeks, and at the base of her throat, pulses of both of them hammering with the shock of release and desire.

Then, just as quickly, he let her go.

She was crying.

Trembling, he took her hand. 'Oh, Kate,' he said. 'Kate. What have we done to each other?'

She shook her head dumbly.

He guided her to a flat slab of granite at the base of the Folly and eased her down, then passed her a handkerchief. 'Dry your eyes, darling. I'm sorry. It just proves–'

'What?'

He smiled bleakly. 'Men are men and women are women. Both with weaknesses. I wanted you here because I wanted – *demanded* the impossible. Proof of your fidelity. But proof doesn't matter any more.' He knew she'd never realize what it cost him to say that. 'I love you, whatever has been, whatever you are. We're going home now, to live as ordinary a life as possible with the children, and I'll never refer to that damned unspeakable incident again.'

'But Rick–' Her voice faltered. 'That isn't enough. You should know – you *must,* that I've told you all the time the *real truth.* I was never *never* unfaithful to you with Jon. *Never* – not physically. It's only been you. Can't you believe it? Even *now?*'

'At this moment perhaps – yes. But tomorrow? – who can say? Some things lie too deeply in memory, Kate, to be completed erased. I'll do my damnedest to squash any shadow if it comes up, and I'll not refer to the incident again. That I can promise. So' – his firm lips curved with a hint of his old charismatic smile – 'what about it? Shall we start afresh? Drive the cobwebs away in a clean sweep? Do you care for me sufficiently?'

She gave a little cry and reached towards him. He lifted her up again and they stood together close, arms entwined, her head resting on his breast below a shoulder.

A curious peace seemed to fill the air, enveloping all around them. Later when they'd recovered from emotional reaction both knew it would be different. Passion would reclaim them after exhaustion had spent itself. But for the moment awareness of reunion was sufficient.

Presently they turned and took the quickest route back to Woodgate.

And it was then that the miracle occurred.

Kate had already gone upstairs, and Rick was taking his boots to the kitchen quarters when he heard voices at a side door. Voices with a familiar tone about them. Curious suddenly, he went to investigate.

One of the maids was in conversation with a woman and a young boy. The woman was swarthy-faced, hawk-nosed, wearing a black shawl over a multi-coloured dress and beads, and with long gold rings swinging from her ears below a red headscarf. The boy too was very dark, curly-haired and good-looking. There was evidently an argument going on. The maid, who was comparatively new at Woodgate, was protesting and trying to close the door, the woman was holding up something that looked like a pendant dangling from a slender golden chain.

Rick recognized her instantly.

'Ah! – Thisbe,' he cried, stepping forward quickly.

There was a flash of white teeth in the wrinkled lean face.

'Mr Ferris, sir. I'm glad to see thee. There's something of yours here.' She pushed the trinket towards him, obviously eager for his response. Rick told the servant to go, and took the chain from the gypsy. After only a few seconds' examination he stared at her in bewilderment.

'Yes. It was once my grandmother's, but when we married I gave it to my wife. I can't understand how you came by it. But you'd better come inside where we can talk.'

Once in the hall, the woman was voluble in her explanation which was interjected by occasional Romany phrases.

'We only got to the forest yesterday, Mr Ferris, sir,' she said, and it was my grandson here, Dirk, who found it.'

'*Found* it? Where? When?'

'Early this morning, sir. He was collecting wood near that hut place that had the pictures in it, and the pool where the poor *rawni,* the lady who did them, was drowned–' She paused.

'The Tree Studio, you mean?'

'Yes, yes. Being a good *chavi* he brought it straight to me, and I saw your name on the back of the pretty thing. See, sir?'

The locket was shaped like a heart. A single small diamond glinted from its centre, and on the back the name 'Ferris' was engraved. He could not recall when Kate had last worn it, and was puzzled that she had left it at the studio. The chain was wrenched, so obviously it had caught on something and fallen off.

He was ruminating over the question when Thisbe, seeing his bewilderment, suggested, 'It must've been there for months, sir, gone into the earth like, and been trampled over since that day of the fight.'

Rick was startled. 'The fight? *What* fight?'

'When that high-and-mighty, yellow-haired *rai* who fancies himself lord of everything, attacked your lovely lady, sir. I saw it all. A real tussle it was – I was behind that big holly tree, sir, and couldn't be seen. Collecting a special kind of herb I was. If the struggle'd've gone on I'd've taken a hand in it. But I'm not young, sir, and it was soon over – when the other lady appeared – the strange one.'

Rick had gone very pale.

'Are you all right, sir?' the gipsy woman enquired, 'is there something wrong in what I've said?'

He pulled himself together. 'No – no. You've done me a great service, Thisbe, and your grandson. Thank you, boy. The pendant means something very special to me, and nothing I can give you in return can repay you.' He put his hands in his pocket and drew out two sovereigns. 'But here's a little of something to show my gratitude – one for you and one for the lad. Dirk you say his name is. Here Dirk.'

The boy glanced at his grandmother questioningly. The brown of her skin appeared to have darkened with a more rosy tinge. 'We don't ask payment for doing what's right,' she said, 'but when a gift's offered by a fine Gorgio gentleman ted'n our way to refuse. So if Mr Ferris wants, you c'n take it in y's own hand, *chavi*.' And to Rick, 'May the blessing of our tribe rest on y'r head, sir, and those of your family for all the moons of your life–'

The boy accepted the coin staring at its gold shine wonderingly, watched by Thisbe's eagle eye. Then, after her slipping the other into a small embroidered bag hanging from her waist, there was a show of signs from one lean arm accompanied by utterings in a strange tongue, good wishes and further thanks from Rick who had been familiar with Thisbe's gipsy clan for many years, and learned to respect them.

Then, still bowing and gesticulating the two figures turned and at a quick speed were soon hurrying down towards the lane and their forest encampment.

For a minute, following their departure, Rick stood perfectly still as though all movement in him had suddenly petrified, trying to absorb the full impact of the gipsy's revelation, which meant that Kate's complete innocence *was* proved, and Jon's accusation had been no more than a dastardly lie.

Unconsciously, his fist tightened over the trinket. He came to life suddenly, turned, and rushed along the hall and up the stairs, taking two at a time, to the bedroom where he knew Kate would be waiting for him and tidying herself for their light lunch.

She was standing silhouetted by the window when he went in, looking like a figure from an impressionist's painting in a frilly white underskirt and camisole, holding a dress of buttercup yellow, about to slip it over her head. The discarded attire she'd worn for her walk to Brad Hill lay casually rumpled on the bed; her pointed, damp, black boots stood at the door for the maid to collect later. The tips of her bare toes peeped provocatively from beneath the skirt, giving an illusion of some enchanting wood-nymph about to run away.

She turned quickly, hearing the door open, followed by the click of a key turning, eyes wide and staring. Although she'd expected him, seeing him there, a ripple of shock and excitement shook her.

'Hello,' she said, like a child taken off-guard. 'I was just–' She attempted to pull the dress over her head, but Rick halted her by stepping quickly forward and making a gesture to help her with the rustling silk.

'Allow me,' he said.

She glanced up at him, and the next moment he'd pulled the gown from her grasp and thrown it across the room.

'Oh, Kate – Kate,' he murmured. 'At last.' The firm sweet curves of her were warm against him as he lifted her up and carried her to the bed. 'You're so lovely. God! how I've missed you.' His lips sought her mouth, her breasts and all the secret feminine valleys of her pulsing body. The hunger of separation was fulfilled and became a fire satisfied.

They lay at length at peace, her head on his breast in the curve of his arm against one shoulder.

When a maid knocked on the door half an hour later to say lunch was waiting, Rick roused himself sufficiently to call out in reply, 'My apologies. We shan't want anything to eat until dinner tonight. I forgot to tell you – we had a bite out.'

'You liar, Rick,' Kate whispered, when the girl had gone. He grinned, and bit the lobe of her ear gently. 'Probably a better one than you are, darling; I should have believed what you said about Jon from the very beginning.' He roused himself as memory registered, got up and reached for his shirt. 'My God! when I see him again I'll give him the hiding of his life. He'll wish he'd never been born.'

'No you won't,' Kate told him. 'There's going to be no violence between the Ferrises and Wentworths.'

'And who says so, madam?'

'*I* do,' Kate affirmed. 'Besides he's in America, remember?'

'Ah! of course. And if what rumour says is true about to get linked up with Carcodale's horsy-looking daughter. Well, maybe that'll prove punishment enough.'

'Stop thinking of revenge,' Kate said, 'only unhappy people want that, and we're not unhappy, are we?' She jumped out of bed, and they stood facing each other until his lips were once more on hers, and he held her silently for a few seconds before agreeing. 'No. Dear love – no. At the moment, I'd say we were the happiest couple in the world.'

And by heaven, he thought, he'd do his best to keep it that way although there might still be a few little tussles ahead.

That was life.

Epilogue

A week later Emily called at Woodgate with something to show Kate and Rick.

A photograph.

It was of a baby with hair as fair as that of Blanche-Rose who could have been her twin except for the old-fashioned clothes.

'Walter would have me bring it when I found it; it was in a box of old photographs,' she said proudly. 'Would you believe it?' She laid it beside one of the new baby lying on a nearby table. 'Aren't we alike? I had hair just as light as hers when I was a child. So we know who she takes after. Of course I was a bit larger. Bigger bones, I expect. And she'll be better looking than me when she's grown. Still–' She broke off with a gratified reflective look on her homely face.

'So long as she remains herself – just Blanche-Rose,' Kate remarked, 'that's all that counts.'

'Don't forget the Ferris bit,' Rick reminded her.

'As if I could with you around.'

They smiled at each other – a secret intimate smile – and Emily knew that all was well at Woodgate.

The publishers hope that this book has given you enjoyable reading. Large Print Books are especially designed to be as easy to see and hold as possible. If you wish a complete list of our books please ask at your local library or write directly to:

Magna Large Print Books
Magna House, Long Preston,
Skipton, North Yorkshire.
BD23 4ND

This Large Print Book for the partially sighted, who cannot read normal print, is published under the auspices of

THE ULVERSCROFT FOUNDATION